13'

Epic Fail

Epic Fail

Cristy Watson

James Lorimer & Company Ltd., Publishers
Toronto

James Lorimer & Company Ltd., Publishers acknowledges the support of the Ontario Arts Council (OAC), an agency of the Government of Ontario, which in 2015–16 funded 1,676 individual artists and 1,125 organizations in 209 communities across Ontario for a total of $50.5 million. We acknowledge the support of the Canada Council for the Arts, which last year invested $153 million to bring the arts to Canadians throughout the country. This project has been made possible in part by the Government of Canada and with the support of the Ontario Media Development Corporation.

Cover design: Shabnam Safari
Cover image: iStock

Library and Archives Canada Cataloguing in Publication

Watson, Cristy, 1964-, author
  Epic fail / Cristy Watson. JUL 3 1 2018

(SideStreets)
Issued in print and electronic formats.
ISBN 978-1-4594-1237-8 (softcover).--ISBN 978-1-4594-1247-7 (EPUB)

    I. Title. II. Series: SideStreets

PS8645.A8625E65 2017   jC813'.6   C2017-903306-9
                                                C2017-903307-7

Published by: Distributed in Canada by: Distributed in the US by:
James Lorimer &   Formac Lorimer Books   Lerner Publisher Services
Company Ltd., Publishers   5502 Atlantic Street   1251 Washington Ave. N.
117 Peter Street, Suite 304 Halifax, NS, Canada   Minneapolis, MN, USA
Toronto, ON, Canada   B3H 1G4   55401
M5V 0M3   www.lernerbooks.com
www.lorimer.ca

Manufactured by Friesens Corporation in Altona, Manitoba, Canada in July 2017.
Job #234943

*This book is dedicated to my Mom and Dad.
I am now working on my seventh book because
you believed in my writing and continued to
encourage me over the past seven years.
Thank you for always cheering me on!
This story is also dedicated to all the youth who see
themselves reflected in the characters of Kenzie and
Jared. Stay strong — you are my superheroes!
In memory of my uncles: Jess and Mario Martinez
(fellow authors) and Don Wheeler. Also thinking
of my cousin Cathy — you are all missed dearly
by our families.*

Jared's Dream

As I sleep, I dream.

I'm with my two best friends, Bree and Kenzie. It's Halloween and we're about nine years old. We're dressed as our favourite X-Men. Bree is Rogue, Kenzie is Kitty Pryde and I'm Wolverine. We're laughing and sharing a huge haul of candy. The girls are cracking up at my jokes. Life is good.

Every time I look at Kenzie, she smiles. Now it looks like we're thirteen. But we're still in the same costumes. Bree spends more time taking selfies on her phone than talking with us. But just like when we were younger, we are playing video games. I win every round. I'm the luckiest guy in the world.

Suddenly, it's black all around me. I can't see anything. The girls are gone. I'm by myself on a bus. I don't know where I am or where I'm going. Then it comes back to me. It's October. We're in grade nine.

I've lost the costume. But I know I've lost more than that. What is it? Why can't I focus?

The bus bumps over a sinkhole and the jolt makes me bite my tongue. I went to town to see a movie. But my insides are shaking so hard I can't keep my knee from bouncing. Everyone on the bus is wearing heavy winter clothes, but I'm sweating. My sweatshirt sticks to my coat. And it's raining inside the bus.

Why didn't I stay at the party? I know what my Grade Twelve asshole brother and his buddies have planned for Kenzie and Bree. Panic courses through my body. I think about becoming an

X-Man so I can get to the party in time to stop it.

I see only my reflection in the bus window. I don't look like a superhero. I'm tall and slim with straight, dark hair. My brother Seth has muscles everywhere and wavy, blond hair. But even though he's built like a body builder, my brother is not a superhero!

I stare at my reflection and think about my brother. All I want to do is punch his lights out. I want to punish Seth for having this sick and demented party. But really I am pissed at myself for bailing on my friends.

I can hear my brother's voice saying, ". . . The more girls I nail, the better I'll feel when I win." I'm disgusted to think we have the same DNA running through our veins. I pull the cord to stop the bus. I won't make it to the party on time unless I run the rest of the way.

Like Nightcrawler, I am at my door in seconds. My body is soaked in sweat and my breathing is fast and harsh. I run in through the back door and bolt for the basement.

I find Seth coming out of his room. Bree is behind him, with only a blanket covering her body. I'm too late for Bree. But it doesn't seem to matter. Like she has Xavier's powers to read my mind, she says, "I don't know where Kenzie is. I've been busy." She smiles at Seth as he bends down to kiss her neck. He doesn't break eye contact with me. Vampire-sized teeth disappear into Bree's flesh.

I shiver.

I step toward Bree. "You know there's only one reason for this party, right?"

Bree holds her hand up to stop me. Seth still has a death grip on her shoulder. She says, "I know what the plan was. I'm not as naïve as Kenzie. But I know what I want. If you need to be a superhero, go save her."

Anger rips through my body as Seth laughs. I want to knock him down. But I need to save Kenzie.

I fly up the stairs to the top floor. I'm stepping over kids making out and sloshing booze everywhere. I fling all the doors open as I run down the hall. Then I hear my name. It's barely a whisper. It sounds like it came from the door beside me. I yank open the door and spot Kenzie.

She is on the bed. Tears are streaming down her cheeks. And that asshole Cam is hovering, ready to climb on top of her.

I leap across the room and shove Cam away from Kenzie. He falls off the bed and lands with a crash beside the dresser. He jumps up, but I am too quick for him. In seconds, I've slammed him into the dresser. Cam passes out on the floor. I grab Kenzie into my arms and carry her out of the room. I leap down the stairs, jumping over the partiers on my way to the door.

Relief fills my body. I got to Kenzie in time to save her.

Chapter 1

The Photo

I wake up.

My bed is drenched in sweat. My body is shaking. The dream feels as real as if it just happened yesterday. It always does. I should be jumping out of bed, eager to enjoy a holiday from school. I should be drooling over the smell of bacon coming from my aunt's kitchen for breakfast. I should be looking forward to turkey and gravy for Thanksgiving dinner.

Instead, I can't move.

I dreamed I got to the party in time to save Kenzie.

But that isn't how things went down.

I lie with the covers over my head. They block out the light that streams through the window in my aunt's spare room. I replay the dream in my head.

Almost everything in the dream is true. My brother and his Grade Twelve buddies were competing to see who could have sex with the most Grade Nine girls. They called them *newbie nines*. The only reason they didn't invite grade eights is that sex with girls that much younger than them makes it rape. As if it wasn't rape anyway!

Well, it wasn't for Bree. She admitted she knew what she was getting herself into. She went to the party and took Kenzie anyway. She didn't care about the contest. She didn't care about hurting her best friend.

Kenzie had no clue that the party was all about a contest. She thought it was cool that older guys invited her to a party. She liked that they were paying attention to her. I'm sure that made it easier for Cam to lure her to a room.

Two years ago, full of panic, I ran through the house, searching for Kenzie. I couldn't find her anywhere.

In real life, I didn't get to Kenzie in time.

My pulse races as memories from that night come flooding back. I feel my hands curl into fists. They slam the mattress over and over again.

Kenzie and I had been dating for a month when the party invitation came. And Kenzie chose the party. She chose older guys over coming to a movie with me. She had no idea that the party was a scam. But I did. I bailed on my friends and I failed them.

That night ranks as the worst of my life. Cam took advantage of Kenzie at the party. Mom came home alone that night from Whistler. She had caught Dad cheating on her with a younger woman from work. Seth thinks

I called Mom to stop the party. Since then, my brother's hatred for me has notched up. Now it has epic status, and I have the bruises to prove it.

Mom feels betrayed because I should have warned her about the party. Kenzie feels betrayed because it was my brother's party and I didn't stop it. My folks are divorced, and Seth blames me for that.

For two years I've tried to tell Kenzie I'm sorry. I made a mistake. I sent a text to warn her, but it came too late. I had been upset with Kenzie for calling me a loser when I asked her to come with me instead of going to the party. So I didn't tell her and Bree about my brother's plans. By the time I realized I didn't want Kenzie to be hurt, it was too late.

Mom's voice cuts through my thoughts. She hollers up the stairs, "Jared, your breakfast is getting cold."

"I'll be down in a minute." Fuel might help get my body moving. I have a Socials test to study for. I'll have time on the ferry ride back to Vancouver, but I should put in some time after breakfast.

I roll out of bed. I grab my cellphone and head to the bathroom. I wet down my mop of bedhead, but some strands still stick out at weird angles. I scroll through my messages.

"Shit!"

I drop my phone.

Panic lurches my body forward. I grab the phone off the floor and look at the screen. The picture is still there. It's a Snapchat photo of Kenzie. It must have been taken at the party that night two years ago. Kenzie's eyes are closed.

She's completely naked.

My hands are sweaty, making it hard to hang onto the phone. I know what I should do. For Kenzie. To make sure that bastard Cam pays this time. I should take a screenshot of the photo. But I hesitate. I never want to see Kenzie this way. Vulnerable and alone.

My fingers hover over the photo. Just as I am about to hit delete, the Snapchat image disappears.

As I make my way downstairs, my chest feels tight. A blistering headache squeezes my brain. I still don't understand why Kenzie never told anyone about what happened. Why did she let Cam get away with what he did? Cam wasn't called out for his actions. He got to finish playing rugby for the rest of the season. He graduated as if nothing happened.

But now, maybe that can change. If Kenzie saw the photo, she could take a screenshot and save it. She can use it to prove to everyone what Cam did. And what my brother did, because he planned the contest and the party. And I know the contest isn't over. Seth and his twisted buddies still tally points for getting Grade Nine girls to have sex with them, and for photos they get their "girlfriends" to post. Of course, Seth is at the top of the list. He has been since the party.

I hope Kenzie uses the photo to take down Cam. And I'd love to see Seth crash and burn. Then maybe we can all move forward. And who knows, maybe Kenzie and I might be friends again?

There's just one problem with that plan. Kenzie has avoided me for two years.

Chapter 2

Confrontation

I help Mom with the dishes while Aunt Sylvia stuffs the turkey.

"Jared." Mom uses her *I have something serious to share with you* voice.

She hesitates. "You know how I said living here in Nanaimo was temporary? That I'd move back to the mainland when things settled?"

I nod and grab our dirty plates from the table.

"Well," Mom continues, "I met someone. He's wonderful. Not anything like your Dad . . . Sorry," she says as she puts the clean cups in the cupboard. "I don't mean your Dad's a bad person. I just . . ."

"I know," I say. I remember their last argument. Dad tried to convince Mom that men need variety and spontaneity. He said she shouldn't take it personally. He reminded her that he always came home to her.

I shared the story with my buddy, Mooney. We both loved my Mom's reply: "I'm not a Stepford Wife." We watched the movie about a whole town of men who were totally controlling of women. It's not hard to see where Seth gets it.

Mom has been living with her sister ever since.

I had been holding out hope that Mom would move back to Vancouver. I could spend time at her place and not have to deal with Seth.

She doesn't know how Seth treats me.

She's not there to see the bruises on my arms. She doesn't know how hard it's been to sleep. And now she won't be home to help me work out what to do about Kenzie. I'm on my own.

* * *

I sit on the ferry, heading home from Nanaimo. I have only one thought. How do I check to see if Kenzie knows about the photo? The picture came to me via a username I didn't know. Why would someone send the photo now, two years later?

While I wolf down a takeout White Spot burger and a chocolate shake, I stress over what I should do. What must it be like for Kenzie, living this?

Thinking about Kenzie makes me realize how much I miss spending time with her. Kenzie always laughed at my jokes. She was always . . . just Kenzie.

Then things changed.

Before Grade Nine, Kenzie mostly wore jeans and t-shirts. Then she switched to short skirts and low-cut tops. I could see she was copying Bree's style. I don't know where Kenzie got the money. She and her sister have always been on a tight budget.

It pissed me off seeing her act like Bree. I was into Kenzie just the way she was — easy-going, not trying to flaunt her body.

Since the party, Kenzie seems to dress in sweatpants and loose sweaters all the time. Not that I would know for sure. She's rarely at school. When she is there, she avoids me. I think she avoids everyone.

I decide to call Mooney. Maybe he'll have some ideas about how to tell Kenzie about the photo.

I pull out my cellphone. My thumbs punch out a text message.

Me: Did u see?

Mooney: If you mean the highly suspect photo, yes.

Me: Why would he send it now?

Mooney: U mean Cam?

Me: Yup.

Mooney: I thought Kenzie was copying Bree.
I thought she sent the photo.

Me: Nope. It was Cam.

I wish I was as sure as I sounded. Bree
sends us all nude photos of herself all the
time. She's become a trading sensation, a hot
commodity. She keeps my stupid brother at the
top of the contest. He's number one — number
one asshole, I say. I look back at my screen.
There is a pause with no text. My thumbs roll
over the keys.

Me: So, what should I do? I need to help
Kenzie.

Mooney: Kenzie's not the only 1
compromised in the pic? U r 2.

Me: Shit!

My fist pounds the table and my empty
cup falls to the ground. As I bend to pick
it up, I catch a couple staring at me. Their

little son blasts me with his toy laser gun. It's weeks before Halloween, but he's dressed as Superman. I bet he still thinks he can save Lois Lane.

I jump out of my seat. I feel like I have to move or I will hit someone. I wish my brother were here right now. I'd squeeze my hands around his thick neck.

I think about how dazed I was when the party ended. Mom took it all in with eyes already red and puffy. She began yelling for everyone to get out. It was a frenzy as people tripped over each other to leave. There was puke everywhere. The coffee table was broken. Seth was boiling mad that Mom had come home early.

But the worst part was that I couldn't leave to check on Kenzie. I had to clean things up. When Dad arrived from Whistler (his girlfriend Laurel gave him a ride) our house turned into a shouting match. I hit the sack at 4 a.m. Everything was a blur. It never dawned on me that someone had been using my room.

But Mooney is right. I think about the Snapchat photo. Kenzie was on *my* bed. Anyone who enlarges the picture will be able to tell. Hanging above my bed is my stupid Tech Award from Grade Seven with my name, Jared Archer, in bold letters.

I head for the outer deck of the ferry. There is a spot where the wind is so fierce you can hardly move forward. I stand with the cold air blasting me. Water is streaming down my cheeks. It must be the wind.

When I go back inside the ferry, I feel better. I have a plan. I will send Kenzie a text saying that we should talk, and that I am her friend. If she responds, I'll figure out what to say next.

I try to study for the last part of the trip home but I can't focus. I'm supposed to call my dad to pick me up. But if he's busy with Laurel, he'll send Seth. I can't deal with my brother right now. So I catch the bus. It takes an hour and a half to get home. Like the long ride I took two years ago, it gives me way too much time to think.

At home, I dart in the back way. I take the stairs three at a time to the rec room in the basement.

Seth's music is blaring. He probably has Bree with him. She has no clue. Since the party, I've seen Seth bring home a parade of girls. There are probably loads more I don't see.

I bang on his door. "Seth, you bastard! Show your ugly face!"

The door swings open. Seth places a huge hand on each side of the doorframe. It works. One, it keeps me from seeing who is in his room with him. Two, it gives the impression of power. No, it actually gives him power.

I shrink back a few steps. What brilliant comment had I planned to make? "Why the hell did you do it?" I finally spit out. "Why didn't you just invite girls *your* age? And where is your jerk friend, Cam?"

"What are you blubbering about now?"

"I'm not . . . I just . . . Shit!" I really want to lay into him. But as usual, I freeze.

Seth drops one hand from the doorframe and places it on my shoulder. He squeezes hard. I feel my eyes water. "For two years you've kept your mouth shut about the contest," he says. "So no one can call out me, Cam, or the other guys. And you know the girls wanted us. So, keep quiet and I'll let you off easy . . . this time."

Before I can respond, Seth slams the door in my face. It nearly takes my nose off. I push my shirt collar aside and look at my shoulder where his hand was. The skin is red. There will be another bruise. I shuffle upstairs.

I crawl under the covers and take my cell from the nightstand. I punch out a quick message to Kenzie:

I care about you. Text me back.

I try to relax. But my mind is full of

images of Kenzie struggling to fend off Cam in my bed — this bed. I feel sick to my stomach. I take my blanket and pillow to the living room and crash on the couch.

It's after 2 a.m. when I finally close my eyes.

Chapter 3

Breaking In

Tuesday morning and I'm at school. I want to turn around and go back home. My head is killing me from lack of sleep. As the bell rings, I text Kenzie. She didn't respond to my message yesterday. I don't know if she has even seen the photo.

I walk down the hall toward the science lab. I have this creeped-out feeling, like people are staring at me. What the hell? I turn to one guy who is grinning. "What's your problem?"

"No problem, dude. Your girlfriend is hot."

I guess he saw the picture of Kenzie. There are probably a hundred things I should say to the jerk. But all I reply is, "She's not my girlfriend."

In Biology, a girl named Sam moves her chair away from me. Later, I see her scrawling words across her lab book: *Asshole. Perv. Prick.*

So now the school thinks *I* did that to Kenzie? Do they have short memories? Half of them were at the stupid party. If they weren't, the rumour mill should have given them the message it was Seth, Cam and the other jerks. I had nothing to do with the contest. But I guess they now know it was my room. It seems like that changes everything.

I wish Kenzie had told the cops, or anyone, what had happened that night. My brother and Cam might have been charged for having the contest. They would have been called out for holding the party. Then Kenzie could have moved on.

But she isn't at school today. Even if she were here, she would be like a zombie. I know this has affected her. But, it doesn't *have* to be this way. Kenzie found out Bree knew what was going to happen. Bree took her best friend along anyway. Kenzie doesn't hang with her anymore. Kenzie should make new friends who have her back. She should get on with her life.

Maybe then she could forgive me.

But Kenzie has shut me out. Now all those people who think I had something to do with what happened that night will feel justified. All the proof they need is in the photo.

I know what I need to do.

I skip the last block before lunch. Kenzie's sister Callie will be at work. She can't keep me from seeing Kenzie like she has for the past two years. If Kenzie doesn't answer the door, I know where they used to keep the spare key. Breaking in isn't my usual M.O., but I will if I have to. I need to see Kenzie. We need to talk.

I run most of the way to her house. I bang on the door. I can see how my anger about the party and the photo might make it hard for Kenzie to hear me out. So I take a few deep breaths. I try to calm my pounding heart.

There is no answer to my knock. I bolt to the rear of the house and hammer on the back door. I wait. Again, no answer.

Their barbecue is off to the side of the deck. I reach under the black cover to the low platform where the propane tank sits. I find a silver key.

I hesitate. Maybe this is the wrong way to handle things. But then my anger flares again. I bang on the door, giving Kenzie another chance to open it up.

After what seems like a half hour, I push the key into the door handle. It turns and I open the door. I don't enter right away. Instead, I call out to Kenzie. There's something other than anger in my voice now, but I'm not sure what it is.

I wait several moments before I venture into the house. It is just like I remember it. The house belongs to Kenzie's grandma, who passed away when Kenzie was two. Callie pays the bills and keeps an eye on Kenzie. Kenzie's mom bailed on them when Kenzie was thirteen, choosing some guy she barely knew over her daughters. I always wondered how she could forget to be a mom. And Kenzie never knew her dad. We figure he went back to live on the reserve in Kamloops.

I head into the kitchen. I recall how we used to make grilled cheese sandwiches and root beer floats. I smile at all the fun we had back in Grade School. It was so much easier when we were young. Suddenly, a piercing scream rips through the house. I freeze. My hands are behind me, clenching the kitchen sink. Kenzie is in pajamas, standing in the hallway. She is staring at me.

"Jesus, Jared," she says. "You scared the hell out of me. What are you doing here?"

"Isn't it obvious?" I step toward her, but she backs up against the wall.

Her eyes dart sideways, like she's planning her escape route.

I step back and lower my hands. I pretend I'm talking to the ten-year-old version of Kenzie. "I didn't mean to scare you. I just want to talk."

Her eyes brim with tears. She slumps down the wall to a sitting position on the floor.

My anger fades. Now I just want to help my friend. My movements are slow as I slide down to sit on the hardwood floor beside her. Kenzie doesn't stop me. But she doesn't look my way. And she doesn't say anything.

"I miss you," I whisper.

A tear runs down her cheek.

Since Kenzie is quiet, I go on. "I didn't mean for any of this to happen. The party — I'm sorry. I texted you. How come you didn't return my call? I went to the party to look for you. But I didn't see you until you were getting into your sister's car. I know . . . that I was too late."

Kenzie bites her lip and turns her face toward me. Anger flames in her eyes. Then she lashes out, "You're *sorry!* Like that changes anything. Words don't make the actions go away, Jared. And now, that messed-up photo shames me all over again. Do you know that after two years I was finally ready to talk about that night? I was finally ready to start putting it all behind me."

I am surprised, but happy at the same time. I can see how much she's suffered. I know that talking about it would probably make the pain go away. "Good for you," I say, and I mean it. But she abruptly stands and shuffles away from me. I follow her to the living room, where she curls up in a chair. She tucks her feet under her and clutches a pillow to her chest.

I'm not saying the right things. Before I know it, Kenzie has shut me out again.

Chapter 4

Spoiled Fruit

I hear the bubbling of Kenzie's fish tank. There it is, sitting in the corner of the living room where it has always been. But the water is a murky mess. I scan for signs of dead fish but they all seem to be alive. Kenzie used to be really proud of the fish tank. She cleaned it all the time and had names for all her pet fish. Now she and the tank kind of resemble each other. I shudder.

"Look, Kenzie," I say. I try to connect

with her eyes but her head is lowered. Her black hair, streaked with green, spills over her face. "I've missed our friendship. I never wanted to see you get hurt. I only knew what my brother's plans were. I didn't want this to happen to you. I never expected you and Bree to even go to the party."

Kenzie looks up at me. The pain in her eyes scares me. Her gaze is so intense I have to look at the floor. She says, "But you *did* let it happen, Jared. And then you turned on me."

"What?" I ask. "What do you mean? I didn't —"

Kenzie cuts me off. "You could have called the cops. Told your parents your brother's plan. Anything. But you didn't. You slunk off to some show and texted me, hoping that would change things. You just wanted to make it better for you."

She lowers her gaze and squeezes the pillow as she goes on. "Then I tried talking to you one day at school. It was just before

Remembrance Day. I thought if you and I could talk, maybe it would help me find the courage to do what I needed to do . . . tell the school counselor. But I saw the look in your eyes. It was a look of disgust over what had happened. It was at that moment I knew I couldn't talk to you. It was then I knew things were different for us. You'll always see me as the girl from that night."

"That's not true!"

Kenzie pulls her legs closer to her chest. Tears stream down her cheeks. Before I can think of what else to say, she continues. "I'm like the spoiled fruit at the grocery store. I'm bruised and dented — and everyone wants perfect fruit. No one will ever want to be with me again."

I have to make her see why I'm there. "If I did look at you the wrong way after that night, I didn't mean to. I wanted you to talk to someone right after it happened. But you didn't. Now, it's starting all over again. And it's affecting both of us." Even as I say the words, I regret them.

Kenzie yells, "Right, it's still about you!"

I'm having trouble saying what is on my mind. But I'm really bugged about Kenzie's comments on how I seemed to her. I know I was confused. Maybe that's what she saw on my face? I don't tell her I'm still a virgin, but I do say, "Kenzie, maybe my emotions were screwed up that night. Before the party, I thought you and I might be together. You know . . . each other's firsts. But discovering you were with Cam messed me up."

She flies out of the chair toward me, stopping a few inches from my face. "I wasn't WITH Cam. Get that straight! I did not sign up for what happened that night." She backs off, but anger still colours her voice. "You know, at one point I thought I wanted to date Cam. But with my naïve schoolgirl crush, I thought that meant walks, movies, parties and kissing." She shakes her head.

"So why couldn't you have accepted those things from *me*? I would have taken you to dinner and out for a show. I would have kissed . . ." I stop before I say something that might be misunderstood. And in the pause, I realize that Kenzie's right. If we got together, I would always be reminded of that bastard, Cam.

As my fists clench, I know I'm not over being angry with Kenzie for going to the party. Because if she hadn't, none of this would have happened.

I pace the room while I try to calm down.

After a long silence, Kenzie lowers her voice. "God . . . maybe I'm more like Bree than I realize. A part of me really just wanted to be seen with Cam. I wanted people to see me and say, 'She's Cam's girlfriend.' Crazy, right?" Kenzie drops her hands from her hips and skulks back to the chair.

I mull over her words. I'm not sure what to make of them. I am angry with her for saying she chose Cam so she could be noticed. But it also makes me sad. Why couldn't she have been happy with us hanging out?

I try to lighten the tension. "You definitely wouldn't have had that kind of fame with me!"

She doesn't laugh and is no longer looking my way. I feel the wall going up again. It seems even heavier than before.

"I got it wrong," I continue, my voice softer. "I just wish we could go back . . ."

"Only if it means I don't go to the party."

"I would make sure of that! I wouldn't go to the movie without you. And even if it meant my brother would pummel me, I'd tell someone." I realize that is part of what stopped me from fixing this two years ago. Stupid pride, and fear of what my brother would do to me.

Is Kenzie right? Maybe I was looking out for myself. That feeling I had earlier, when I arrived at Kenzie's house, maybe it's guilt? My shoulders slump. I realize how stale the air is in the living room.

Kenzie stops me as I cross the room to open a window. "It doesn't matter now, Jared. It happened! And it's happening all over again. That bastard, Cam."

"But a few minutes ago you said you were ready to talk about it. Were you going to confront Cam?"

"Hell, no! I was going to tell the school counselor, or maybe the cops. My sister has been nagging me for two years to deal with this. She's worried all the time. She stays home from work to keep me company when I'm having a bad day. I don't want her to lose her job. She's been holding us together for so long. Then last week, I got brave. I decided it was time to tell my story."

I figure if she had told someone, especially the police, I would have heard about it. Or I would have felt the truth inflicted on me by Seth, as he used me for a punching bag. But I hadn't heard a thing.

"So what happened?" I ask.

Kenzie looks at me. I notice how her brown eyes no longer have the spark of life they used to. It's like she is wearing a veil over them. It's like she is in front of me, but not really here. Over the past two years she's been absent from school tons of times. Looking at her now, I can see it's like she's been absent from life. But a week ago, she was ready to make a positive change. To take charge of her life again.

All before the photo surfaced.

Chapter 5

Guilty Party

"Okay, Kenzie, so you follow through," I say. "The photo is just further proof that Cam is a total creep."

I think about what Mooney said. Seeing Kenzie this way, I know for certain she didn't post the photo. My brother seemed pretty sure Cam didn't do it, even though he is a lying son-of-a-bitch. If Cam and my brother didn't have anything to do with this, who did?

"You don't get it," says Kenzie. She moves to the curtain and peeks through. Then she closes it and sits on the floor in front of the chair. She picks at her nails.
But she doesn't say anything. I want to fill the silence, to apologize again, but I can't make the words come.

Finally Kenzie speaks. "For a long time, I thought it was all my fault. Truth is, I still think that. My sister has been trying to convince me that to get better, I need to talk with someone. I need to tell someone what happened that night."

I wonder what she means by "get better." I assume she means missing school. I hadn't really noticed until now, but she has crater-sized dark circles under her eyes that her long bangs barely hide. She has gained some weight. Now that I really look, I can see that stress has had an impact on her.

"I lost my voice that night," Kenzie says. "I couldn't say *NO*, loudly enough. Cam was drunk and didn't hear me then, so why would anyone have listened to me afterward?"

"I hear you," I say. I want to move beside her and take her hand. But I know I am better off keeping a safe distance. A distance that is safe for her.

"No, you don't. You are here because you want me to forgive you. For two years you have been all about *your* needs. You say you wish you told me sooner. You wish you were there to stop it. But you didn't do those things. You are guilty of betraying your friends and you want the guilt to go away. Now that the photo has emerged, I don't know if you are here to help me or to make sure no one thinks it was you who did it. You just want to cover your ass!"

"Christ, Kenzie! Cut a guy some slack. Maybe I haven't gone about things the right way. But I really am sorry it happened."

"Forget it. If you can't even name it, why talk about it? I was RAPED by Cam at *your* brother's party. Plain and simple. But no one will see it that way. They'll see a desperate girl who wanted to fit in with the social climbers. They'll see a girl who put on makeup and a short skirt and went to a party, hoping the older guys would pay attention to her. Well she got more attention than she ever wanted. End of story!"

Kenzie stands up. She stomps off toward the bathroom on the main floor. Before she slams the door in my face, I manage to say, "But it doesn't have to be the end of the story. Let's figure out who sent the photo. Let's take them down, along with Cam and my brother. I'll help you!"

For the next ten minutes there is nothing but silence between us. Kenzie doesn't come out of the bathroom. I have run out of things to shout through the door. I finally leave when I realize she isn't going to talk to me.

I jog to the McDonald's on 152nd Street on my way back to school. After I eat, I feel better. I'm still stressed by everything that happened at Kenzie's place. But the food seems to have settled my nerves. I check my messages. Nothing from Kenzie. But there is a text message I missed from Mooney. It says:

Where the hell r u? SS Test?

Shit! I totally forgot about the Social Studies test. The class will be over by the time I get back to school. Maybe I can fake the flu and say I was sick. Would McDougall believe I just went home without telling anyone? Will he let me do the test another time? I doubt it.

I decide to bail on school. The house is empty when I get home. Seth works at Canadian Tire, so that must be where he is. I pour myself a glass of juice and sit down in the living room. I'm just about to turn on the TV when I hear a noise coming from downstairs.

My chest heaves as all the air vacates my lungs at once. I take small steps toward the door that leads to the basement. Seth's motorbike isn't in the carport, so he's not home. Dad is at work. Maybe Laurel came over? But then wouldn't her Mazda be parked on the street?

I place a toe on the first step. I grab the rail so I can move without alarming the intruder. I wish I had grabbed Seth's baseball bat from the hall closet.

I barely breathe as I reach the bottom step. As I look into the rec room, I see Seth's door is open and the light is on. Then I hear a familiar voice. "I know these aren't my panties. Wait until I get my hands on that jerk!"

Bree flies out of my brother's room and slams into me.

"What the hell?" she screeches.

"More like, WHAT THE HELL!!!" I yell back. "You're the person breaking and entering. Sneaking into my brother's room. What's your problem?"

"Your asshole brother is the problem."

"I told you that two years ago, but you didn't listen. You just do your own thing, not giving a shit about anyone else. Do you even know what you did to Kenzie?"

"Hey, Kenzie was just as eager to party as I was. That's on her, not me." Bree tries to move around me, but I block her way.

"You really are a bitch, Bree. Kenzie has been trying to sort things out ever since that night. She was finally ready to fix things. And then that stupid photo surfaced."

"Yeah. Fix things. She would have brought me down with her. That's why posting the photo was brilliant. I . . ."

Bree looks at the ground. It takes me a moment to realize what she just said. As I try to figure out what she means, she squeezes around me. I watch her bolt up the stairs. I hear the front door slam. I replay her words in my head until I am sure I have it right.

Bree posted the picture of Kenzie?

For the second time in two days, I am faced with a dilemma. What do I say to Kenzie? Do I even tell her that it was Bree who posted the pic? Maybe I can find a way to start a smear campaign against Bree. The only positive thing out of this is that Bree now knows my brother was sleeping around on her. I wonder who tipped her off.

I head to my room and lie on my bed. I scroll through my phone, opening my photos. Over the years, I've uploaded nearly 300 pictures. There are pictures of the Halloween we dressed up as characters from *Harry Potter*. Of course, I was Harry. Bree was Hermione and Kenzie was Ginny. The next picture shows the three of us around a campfire, roasting marshmallows. It was the time we went to Camp McLean, the scout camp on 16th Avenue, near Langley.

My fingers brush the screen so that photo after photo appears. The pictures show the three of us doing all sorts of crazy things. I see Kenzie dressed up for her tenth birthday party. And there is a picture of the Christmas she and Callie spent at my place. That was the Christmas after her mom bailed. Kenzie is under the tree, her face lit up as she opens a present. She looks happy. We all look happy. But that was before the party that changed everything.

That was before the naked photo of Kenzie popped up all over the Internet.

Chapter 6

The Tap

Wednesday after lunch, I help set up for an assembly in the gym. I didn't get to eat, as I had to write my make-up Social Studies test. Now my stomach is growling. Our AV teacher, Mr. Asuni, taps me on the shoulder. "Hey, Jared, how is it coming along?"

"Nearly done," I say. I plug the XLR cable into the PA. "Just about ready to test the equipment."

"May I?" Mr. Asuni asks. He pushes his

glasses further up his nose and grabs hold of the mic. I move the fader to unity on the input channel. Mr. Asuni taps the mic and says, "Test one, two, three, four. Test, test, test." His voice booms across the school gym.

I tune up the mic trim and then climb down the small step-ladder. As I stand beside Mr. Asuni, I'm looking down on his bald head.

"As always, you are bang on!" Mr. Asuni shakes my hand. Then his voice softens. I lean in so I can hear him. "So, Jared, at the staff meeting yesterday they told us about a new training program. We were asked to think of kids in our classes who do a service to our school. Kids that help out and have positive attitudes. They're not the ones you would typically see joining activities, you know . . ."

I jump in, "You mean popular?"

"Well, yes . . . no, I mean . . . They want kids who could use a boost, but already do good things for our school. Like you. I thought of you right away, Jared. I may not have said this in the best way. But you'd be good at this and other kids would benefit. I really hope you'll give it a try? I kind of told them you'd come."

Great! Forcible engagement — teachers are so good at that! Since he hasn't told me what it is he's tapping me for, I shake my head. "Probably not my deal. But thanks all the same."

"Let me start again," says Mr. Asuni. He wipes sweat from his bald head. "It's a training session for about twenty kids. Over four school days. You miss school but you learn about becoming a Peer Mediator. You know, people who can help others. That's what I meant when I said you'd be good at it."

I'm not sure what gave Mr. Asuni the idea I'd be good at helping other people. I'm not good at crowds, even small ones. I'm part of the AV club because I'm good with electronics. And it means I don't have to deal with anyone else. Besides, trying to help

Kenzie has been an epic failure. I don't say no. But I don't promise anything, either. My stomach is already vaulting into panic mode at the thought of it.

Mooney walks up and says hi to Mr. Asuni, who heads toward the door. "Think about what I said, Jared," Mr. Asuni says. "The meeting is Friday at lunch in the Library."

"What's that about?" Mooney asks. He sets to work helping me hide the cords so that when people come into the gym, they don't trip over them.

"Some club or something he thinks I should join. I don't know. He was kind of cryptic in his description. Something about unpopular kids doing good deeds for the school."

"That's you," Mooney laughs. He climbs a ladder to check the lighting.

"Right. I am a total joiner."

"So, will you really check it out?"

"Yeah, maybe." Then I grin and add, "If you'll join the GSA!"

"What are you talking about?" Satisfied the lights are working, Mooney climbs down to stand beside me. He's wearing his usual outfit, white shirt tucked into grey jeans, topped with a black trilby hat.

"I see how you look at Colin," I say. "Like Seth looks at chicks."

"What? I don't look desperate, pathetic and like a perv!"

We both laugh.

"Okay," I say. "So that didn't come out right. I mean you look like you're interested in him. I'm pretty sure I saw Colin coming out of the GSA meeting last week. Might be a good way to get to meet him?"

"And if my parents find out I've joined a GSA?"

I pat his shoulder. "Then you get to come out to them without all the stress of actually telling them. Look, I know you're scared. But

I really think your mom will be cool with it. Your dad might take some work. But he'll get there, too. You're the only kid I know with a normal family — not divorced or missing in action. Just there. Trust them."

"That's easy for you to say. You're not the one who has to stand in front of them and say the words."

"Okay, so even more reason to join the GSA. They probably talk about how tough it is to tell your parents. I bet they can give you ideas and support."

He nods and places his arm around me. "Okay, but only if you check out the group on Friday."

* * *

When school is over, Mooney and I head to the mall. As we walk, I tell him about what happened with Bree. I'm hoping he'll have ideas for what I should do next.

"She broke in to your house!"

"I guess," I reply. "Unless Seth made her a key. Either way, he wasn't home. And she can't have told him yet." I push the button to cross Johnston Street.

"How do you know she didn't tell your brother?"

"Uh, no new bruises? Seth would have pummeled me if Bree broke up with him. Without Bree, he'll drop from top spot in the frigging contest. I overheard Seth explain it once. The only way guys get points is if they get 'newbie nines' to have sex with them, or if their girls post nude photos."

Mooney asks, "Do you think Bree's plotting revenge? Maybe the photo incident was about that too?"

"Probably." I feel a wave of sadness. "Kenzie finally wanted to tell someone about that night. Her big mistake was choosing Bree. I'm not sure why she even told her. They haven't been hanging out for two years.

So maybe Bree felt threatened? If her lawyer dad found the photos, she'd be in major trouble. Or at least, she wouldn't be allowed to see Seth anymore."

"They're over now, anyway. Aren't they?"

We sit at a table in the crowded food court. We've grabbed slices of pizza. Mooney's choice is chicken with spicy peppers. Mine is the usual, pepperoni. I suck back the coke I got to wash down the pizza. After a good belch, I get serious again. "Okay, so if Bree is the one who posted the photo, do I tell Kenzie? Or should I confront Bree? Or can I just find a way to prove it, so Bree gets caught?"

"I'm for number three," says Mooney. "That skank needs a shake-down."

We spend the rest of the afternoon on the Internet at my place, looking for software to trace Bree's posts. It's easy enough to go through her Facebook and Instagram and check out all the photos she sent us of herself. She is so free with her pictures. Maybe she really thought Kenzie would be, too? But then, I know Bree. Everything is about her.

When I hear Seth's motorbike pull into our carport, I panic. "Mooney, let's chill at your place. I am done dealing with my brother."

Chapter 7

Not a Superhero

Thursday was a write-off. Kenzie didn't come to school. I had to abandon my Internet search on Bree. My phone pinged non-stop. The photo on Snapchat disappeared, but the fallout was huge. It seems the whole school had something to say about the photo. And none of it was nice.

I don't get it. Bree sends nude photos of herself, and people trade and share them. I know that girls have even passed her photos along to other girls. There isn't any backlash against Bree.

Kenzie has no control over what happened to her that night. And now she has no control over the photo being posted. But *she* is a slut? That doesn't make sense. I hope Kenzie doesn't see one really hurtful comment. It says, "Nice tits, if you could put a bag over her head."

I have already blocked twenty-three people so I won't get any more messages from them. A lot of comment are aimed at me. Whether or not people think I hurt Kenzie two years ago, they assume I posted the photo since it shows her in my room.

A steady stream of "asshole," and other nasty messages fill the screen. The worst one reads, "Prick couldn't get it up, so he rams a drunk?"

I don't bother trying to deal with them. If the cowards can't talk about it to my face, they aren't worth the effort. I hope Kenzie has blocked them, too. She doesn't need this crap.

It's Friday and I'm sitting in the library. Mooney convinced me to come. He thought mediation might help me with the current conflict in my life. But what if they all know about the photo?

The set-up in the room freaks me out. Chairs are arranged in a circle. There are no desks or tables. There is a teacher in the room organizing snacks. She says "Hello," while I wait.

I have my head bent over my phone like something really interesting occupies my attention. But it is just to get my nerves under control. A few people walk in and talk with each other. They look like they are in Grade Twelve.

A girl sits down in the chair next to me. I feel nervous. I don't want to talk to anyone. I don't want to be here. I'm about to bail but a calm comes over me as the girl leans in to say "Hi."

She smells like somewhere tropical, like a vacation. It reminds me of the trip our family took to Acapulco when I was young. That helps me calm down enough to stay in the room.

"I'm Jessie," the girl says.

"Hey, I'm Jared." I don't remember seeing her around, so I ask, "Are you new to our school?"

"Yup. Moved here over the summer. The new place is up on 24th."

I think about what to say so I can keep the conversation going. But then a Grade Twelve student asks for our attention.

"I'm Sean. Glad you could make it to our meeting today. As you all know, our school mascot is a Ram, so we call ourselves Restorative Action Mediators. We help students who are in conflict to restore their relationships. Basically, we help them figure out how to fix things."

I look around the room. The students are nodding as Sean talks.

He continues. "So, if you decide to take the four-day training, we'll meet here and do all our work from within a circle. We sit in a circle because it's important to be able to see and hear each other. It makes us more open to one another; more connected. You will learn skills over the next four sessions that will help you become a peer mediator. Then when younger students in our school are in conflict, you can help them sort it out."

I wish I had known about this in Grade Nine. I wonder if peer mediation could have helped Kenzie then. I zone out for a few moments, thinking about the past week. When I tune back in, the teacher is telling us that a *talking piece* is something we use so we all know whose turn it is to talk. The rest of us listen while one person holds the talking piece and shares their story. Ms. Golan says we will introduce ourselves. She wants us to finish this sentence, "Something you may not know about me is . . ."

The talking piece is passed from student to student as they introduce themselves. Okay, I really need to focus. My palms are sweaty and my right knee bounces as my nerves heat up. I listen closely so I can check out what my peers are saying.

A girl named Huda introduces herself. She is a Syrian refugee who has only been in Canada since May. Wow! Her English is amazing for being here such a short time. She must really understand conflict.

I freeze. It will be my turn after Jessie. I haven't a clue what I'm going to say. Jessie says her name. Then she says, "Something you may not know about me . . . is that I just moved to this school and haven't made a lot of friends yet."

Jessie nudges me with her elbow. Right. My turn.

"My name is Jared." I look at the ground. I'm aware of every single person in the room staring at me. That makes it ten Grade-Tens checking out the program, ten Grade-Elevens, including me, and three Grade-Twelves plus one teacher. That's twenty-three pairs of eyes trying to look into mine. All of them are likely wondering if I posted the photo of Kenzie. It's way too intense for me!

Words form in my mouth, but I don't know what I'm saying. I blurt out the next part of the introduction. "Something you may not know about me is . . . that . . . I'm . . . not a superhero."

There are several chuckles and my face burns. Sean reminds everyone there is no judgment in the circle. I keep my eyes glued to the floor. I can't see any of the others' faces. I've just made the lamest first impression as a future mediator ever!

"We're just about finished this meeting," says Hudson, the only other guy whose name I remember. "So, let's end with a game. A game that helps us get to know each other better."

You can feel the relief from the students. Doing a circle is highly stressful. If this is how training will be, I'm not sure I want to keep coming. But when Hudson explains the game, I have to admit it sounds fun.

Jessie is picked to go first. She says, "Big Wind Blows on anyone who . . ." she pauses while we all move to the edge of our seats. I don't want to be stuck in the middle. If what she says is true for me, I will bolt across the circle and jockey with anyone who gets in my way of finding an empty chair. Jessie finishes the game phrase with, ". . . likes curry!"

About half of the people get up with me. I dash across the circle and grab a seat. I can't help myself, I laugh. One student gets caught in the middle without a chair. She says, "Big Wind Blows on anyone who has been to Mexico." There's that Mexico trip again. I hadn't thought about it in years. Along with several people, I get up and move. The next person in the middle is a Grade Eleven student. He looks directly at me, and then says, "Big Wind Blows on anyone who is NOT a superhero!"

Everyone gets up out of their chairs.

Chapter 8

Connected

Mooney and I walk home after the training. I have come up with a plan. I say, "Okay. I know what to do to help Kenzie."

"So what's your idea?"

We are crossing the street as I reply. "Kenzie will come to training with me." I'm grinning from ear to ear.

Mooney stops in the middle of the road. "Bad plan, dude."

"Why? I think it would be perfect. There's

no judgment. Everyone listens to each other. Kenzie will learn ways to make things better."

Cars are honking at us, so we start across the street again.

Mooney says, "Kenzie's too raw right now. Even if people are supportive, talking about it might bring up more pain."

"Yeah, but she doesn't have to talk about *the incident*. She can talk about conflict, you know, in general. How people don't treat each other right, and what to do about getting beyond it. Because she's been bullied, she'll have empathy for other people with similar problems. I mean, wouldn't that help her figure out how to solve what's going on with her?"

We pass the mall entrance and continue on to White Spot. There isn't a line so the server seats us right away. We decide on burgers and put in our order. Then Mooney lowers his voice and says, "I don't think Kenzie will see what happened to her that night as bullying. It's date rape. That goes a lot deeper."

He leans in. "I do think you have a point, bro. Kenzie needs acceptance, and someone who won't judge her. But she needs it from a friend, not from total strangers. The stuff you're learning will help *you* help Kenzie. I think it's a bad idea to put her in that session. It won't matter if people are judging her or not, she'll feel judged anyway. She feels judged now."

I shrug my shoulders. My milkshake arrives and I slurp it through the straw. Okay, Mooney disagrees with my idea. But deep down I believe it's the right thing.

When tomorrow comes I will head to Kenzie's and give her the news.

* * *

I decide to ignore Mooney's warning. After lunch on Saturday, I head to Kenzie's house. I knock on the front door, hoping Callie isn't home. To my surprise, Kenzie opens the door after only a few moments.

"Hey, Jared," she says. She invites me into the kitchen and we sit at the table. "Callie stayed with her boyfriend last night, so we're alone."

She brings us both glasses of ice water. And then she says, "I'm sorry."

"What are you sorry for?" I ask. "It was my fault, coming here and reminding you of everything."

"I don't need reminding. It's with me every day. No, I was angry and unleashed all my pent up emotions on you. It felt good to get some of it out. But my real anger is at Cam."

"Better than at yourself," I add.

"Oh, believe me, there has been plenty of anger to go around. And I directed a lot of it at myself. Actually . . ." She looks out the window. I notice that the curtains are now open. "I shouldn't have blocked you out, Jared. Maybe I wouldn't have been so hard on myself then." She bites her nail.

"Well, I was a jerk," I say. "And what you

said before, I thought about it. You're right. I was all about getting rid of my own guilt. I wasn't there for you when I should have been."

Kenzie grabs a bag of chips from the counter and opens it. She eats several handfuls then says, "Listen, the photo brought it all back to the surface. Every ugly detail from two years ago. I need time. Someday, I want Cam to know how this affected me. But I don't think I can tell anyone right now . . ."

"You have to! You're so close."

"I don't *have* to do anything. At least that's one thing I learned from all of this."

"Yeah . . . but listen. I have something that will help. It will make a difference." I take her hand and lead her to the living room. Her fish tank is still thick with dirty water and algae. "Let's clean your tank while we talk. I bet your fish would like some fresh water."

"Oh my god," she says. "You know, I've just been adding fish food. It's weird how I didn't even notice it was that dirty. How gross. I am embarrassed you saw this."

"Hey, you were busy taking care of yourself. Now, with two of us here, we can take care of your fish, too."

We start the huge task of cleaning Kenzie's tank. I tell her about my mom's new boyfriend, and update her on Mooney and school life. I share with her that I'll be taking mediation training. I mention how much fun I had in the first session. Then I suggest that she might want to join as well.

Kenzie plops down in a chair after we finish cleaning the tank. "No, Jared. I mean thanks. But it's not for me. I need time to sort things through on my own." She sits up. "You know, one thing I have been thinking about is . . ."

I cut Kenzie off. I know if she hears me out, she will see that this is the right thing for her. But as I tell her how great it will be, I watch her shrink into her chair. I change my approach, thinking it will give Kenzie a chance to absorb what I'm saying. I know she'll see the logic in my plan.

But she's quiet. She seems to have gone someplace else, someplace inside herself.

I realize I'm doing it again. I'm going at my pace, not Kenzie's. "Okay, I didn't mean to tell you what to do. I just want to help." I stand beside the fish tank and grin. "Doesn't the tank look better?"

Kenzie nods. I wipe my wet hands on my jeans. I check the temperature and find that it's safe to put the fish back in the tank. The fish dart around the plastic trees. They swim in and out of the caves.

"How about the Internet?" I ask Kenzie. "Have you shut that thing down? I hope you aren't checking it all the time."

"And what if I am?" she blurts out. "You're at school. You get to hang with Mooney and your other friends. You get to check out new programs at lunch. What do I get to do?"

"You could come to school. I've got your back. I've got ways to help you."

"It's easy for you, Jared. You weren't the one . . . You don't have people judging you every time you look at them."

"Actually, I've been getting a steady stream of crazy shit on my phone. I've blocked tons of people. And I still get looks as I go down the hall. People think I did this. The picture showed my room."

Kenzie sighs. "The Internet has been my social lifeline for two years, Jared. I can't make myself go to school most days. At least social media lets me feel connected."

"Well, that's half your problem right there. You need to rely on real people — people who care about you."

"Until you knocked on my door I was going it alone. If I turn off the stream, I'll have nothing. I'll die without some connection to the world outside my head."

"You'd rather read bullying taunts than

have peace and quiet? I don't get that."

"Try being home alone with only your thoughts, Jared. If you had my thoughts in your head, you'd look at anything to stop them. No. If you had my thoughts in your head, you'd probably have done yourself in by now."

"That's not funny, Kenzie. Look, I'm here. And I want to hang out some more."

I pull her out of the chair and lead her to the couch so we can sit beside each other. I realize my plan is not working. But I have another idea. We'll travel down a different path of memories. I'll take her back to when we were best friends.

I pull out my phone and start at the beginning of my photo collection.

Chapter 9

Disconnected

"Oh my god," laughs Kenzie.

I forgot how infectious her laugh is. It makes me crack up, too, just like it always has. We are looking at a photo of her in the bunny costume she wore in Grade Four. Bree was Alice, you know, in Wonderland. Kenzie was the White Rabbit. I was the Knave of Hearts.

I haven't said anything about Bree being the one who posted the photo. I wait to see if Kenzie says anything. Maybe she'll tip me off

about whether she knows Bree did it.
But Kenzie just laughs at Bree's costume.

"Bet that was the last time Bree wore a dress that went below her knees and buttoned all the way to her neck!" She shakes her head. "I honestly don't know what I was thinking that night. Following Bree's lead."

"Hey, don't be so hard on yourself. We three were all best friends for years. The good times outweighed the bad stuff. So you trusted her. I'm pissed she betrayed you."

"Yeah, well . . ." Kenzie leans her head against my shoulder. I keep thumbing through the old pictures. But all I can think of is how nice it feels. Kenzie's hair smells freshly washed, like strawberries. I ache for our friendship and our old times together.

Kenzie stops my finger scrolling. A picture of us whitewater rafting comes up. It was the summer before Grade Nine. It was the first time I asked her out on a date. It was when our friendship changed to something more serious.

"Wait. I want to look more closely at this one." She sits up and takes my phone. As she looks at the picture she says, "This is brilliant. I feel like writing a poem to capture an idea that just popped into my head. This is the old me, the one who was scared to death of going in that raft. Remember how you held my hand to get me into the boat? I almost couldn't do it. I wouldn't have done it if you hadn't hung on to me."

"It was a blast," I say. "Even though every time I looked at you, your face was dead white. I'd never seen your eyes so huge. The relief on your face when it was over . . . Remember how you laughed like crazy all the way home? Your whole face lit up, because you survived something that scared the hell out of you."

"You know," Kenzie says, "it's kind of like what I'm going through right now. It's like the past two years have been a bumpy ride on a whitewater raft down some crazy river. A ride that no one would ever take if they knew the dangers. I feel like the rapids have gone over my head so many times that I won't ever see the shore again. I feel like I've been drowning. Like I won't ever make it to calm waters where I can just breathe."

"Wow, that *would* make a good poem. I didn't know you liked writing."

"I didn't, either." She laughs. Then she enlarges the photo. After a few moments, Kenzie asks if she can send the picture to herself. Then she turns to me and her eyes are brimming with tears. "Why the hell would someone post that photo of me now? Why couldn't they just let things be?"

Her mood has changed, just like that. Kenzie asks to be alone. I'd rather stay, but she insists.

As I leave, the strangest thing keeps popping up in my mind. It's the last thing I saw before leaving the living room.

One fish was lying on its side, floating on

top of the water in Kenzie's tank. Maybe it died because the clean water was too much of a shock.

Heading home, I replay the events in my head. We were doing okay until Kenzie thought about the photo of her posted on the Internet. Then she shut me out. My pace quickens until I'm running down the street. My arms pump the adrenalin through me. I'm boiling mad. But this time, my anger is directed at Bree. She caused all this shit. It's her fault. Kenzie was finally making progress. And then she was reminded of the photo. I know what I need to do.

I change my course and run all the way to Bree's house. I need to confront her. I bang on the door and Bree's dad opens it. Good thing it's him. Bree probably wouldn't have let me in. Bree's dad welcomes me into the foyer and calls for his daughter to come downstairs.

Bree strolls down the steps to the main floor. When she sees me she says, "Jared, what are you doing here?"

Her dad is standing right there. Bree can't risk that I'll say something. So she grabs my hand and drags me to the garage. Her dad shakes his head. As the garage door closes I hear him say, "Nice to see you, Jared. Come by more often."

Bree chuckles at that. Her sneering laugh is all I need to make me lash out.

"Why the hell did you post the picture?" I ask. "Wasn't it bad enough that you made Kenzie go to the party in the first place? Haven't you hurt her enough?"

"I didn't make anyone go to the party, Jared. Kenzie is her own person. She makes her own choices. Just because she wasn't ready for the big league, it's my fault? Everyone wants to give *me* hell. That's screwed up."

"No, *you're* screwed up. Sending naked photos to all the guys."

"Hey, it keeps me in top spot in the game. Besides," she flips her hair and looks down at her chest, "with a body like mine, why wouldn't I share?"

"You mean," I cut in, "it keeps my brother in top spot. You're nothing more to him than points and rank."

My comment seems to have hit a nerve. Bree's voice is shaky as she replies. "No, it's for me, too. I get to see how many guys check me out. It's kind of like flirting."

"So let me get this straight. It's flirting, but with dudes you don't know and don't have any interest in. Why send all those guys pictures of yourself naked? You don't want to date any of them . . . any of us. Because you're going out with my brother."

"I *was* going out with your jerk brother. He's a waste of time."

"But when you were with him, you were still 'flirting' with other guys." I make air quotes around the word. Even I know that sexting is different from flirting. "Don't you think that's kind of messed up? And then you get mad at Seth for sleeping around on you?" I have to give my head a shake. It sounds like I am defending my brother. And how messed up is that?

"Look," Bree says. "You don't have status. But when I send you a picture of me, well, now you have status. I gave that to you."

"What? Okay, now you're being delusional. I came here to tell you that what you did to Kenzie was unforgivable. Posting the photo of her in that position was humiliating and cruel. We were all friends once. What happened to you? What happened to our friendship?"

As if it is an answer, she replies, "High school."

I sigh. Clearly I am not going to convince Bree that she is wrong. I am not going to be able to help Kenzie mend her friendship with Bree. And that's probably a good thing. Bree is a lost cause.

There isn't any way I am going to get through to Bree. Talking to her will only fuel my anger more.

As I fly out the door, I bump smack into Kenzie. I scramble to keep us both from falling to the concrete sidewalk outside Bree's house.

"What are you doing here?" I ask her.

"I could ask you the same thing," she replies.

"Oh, I was just checking something out. But listen, why don't we go to lunch. Just you and me? My treat." I know I don't want Kenzie to find out what I just learned from Bree. Knowing that someone she thought was her best friend hurt her on purpose would break Kenzie.

Kenzie climbs the last two stairs and raises her arm to knock on the door. I gently pull it down and turn her shoulders to face mine. "Honest, I just want it to be the two of us." I hate that my voice sounds desperate.

Kenzie pulls her hand out of mine and knocks on the door. She says, "Why don't you join Bree and me? Maybe it'll be like the old days. The three musketeers, best friends again, hanging out."

As the door swings open, I am so scared for Kenzie I yell, "You can't go back! It will never be like it was before!"

Chapter 10

Punching Bag

Bree steps out onto the porch. She raises her eyebrows at me. Then she scans Kenzie up and down.

Kenzie says, "Hi." But the strength her voice had a few moments ago is gone. Her voice is now barely a whisper. I don't know what Kenzie thought she'd gain by talking to Bree. And now, Kenzie is shrinking inside herself. She must be wondering the same thing I was.

I have to bail her out. But as I try to

think of something brilliant to say, Bree grabs Kenzie's arm and whisks her into the house.

The door slams in my face, but not before I hear Bree saying, "We don't need that loser."

I knock on the door but no one comes to open it. I would bang on it until Bree opened it, except I know her dad is home. I don't want to embarrass myself — or Kenzie — in front of him.

As I shuffle down the sidewalk, I send Kenzie a message.

Me: Text me when u r done w/ Bree. I'll be at Tim Hortons. Still my treat. C u soon.

I wait but there is no reply from Kenzie.

I head to Tim Hortons and grab a soup and sandwich. I check my messages every few seconds as I eat. An hour passes. Still no Kenzie. Still no message on my phone. I wait for another fifteen minutes and then say to hell with it. I book it home. I don't know how Kenzie will feel if she finds out it was Bree who posted the photo. Maybe it is best for me to give Kenzie some space and try again later.

I head to the kitchen to grab a can of Coke. But I hear voices, so I stop in the hallway, out of view. It's Cam and Seth. They are arguing in the kitchen.

"So *why*, after all this time . . ." Cam says. "Why did you do it, Seth? Why did you post the picture you took two years ago? The one of Kenzie, you know, after we had sex?"

"I didn't do it. Bree did it."

"Bree? Why the hell would Bree send it?"

I can tell my brother is uncomfortable. He mumbles a lame answer.

Cam continues, "Bree posted Kenzie's picture so you could get extra points for that stupid contest?"

I hear a shuffle of feet and the snap of a can opening. There's silence for a few seconds, as someone guzzles a beverage. Then my brother's voice cuts through the air. It's tinged with anger.

"You didn't think the contest was stupid

two years ago," Seth says. "In fact, you seemed to enjoy that night."

"I was hammered after our beer chugging games. So was Kenzie when she came with me to the room. At first, I thought she was okay with everything. By the time I realized she was upset . . . well, it was too late. I messed up! Now I'm trying to get my life back on track so I can register for UBC next year, I want to ask the new girl at my work out for a date. But then the photo . . . Look . . . I just want it all to go away."

Seth's voice is getting louder, like he's heading toward me in the hallway. As I back up so he won't spot me, I knock a vase off the hall table. I catch it in time. *Whew.* The last thing I need is for Seth to catch me listening.

Seth's voice booms. "So, you think you're too good for us now? All the guys? The contest? Are you sure it isn't because you're the reigning champ of *last place* in the contest?"

"Grow up, dude. We were assholes back then. That isn't who I am now."

"So what? You've grown a conscience. So now you're going to advertise what we did?"

"You mean, what you're *still* doing," says Cam. "You go ahead. Keep on being an immature prick. I'm not going to open the wound any further. I'm done with you. I'm done with the contest. I'm done with the past."

Cam storms out of the kitchen and turns right, heading out the front door. I flatten myself against the left side of the wall. I try to go unseen as I fly past the kitchen to the stairs to my room. But Seth's voice stops me dead in my tracks. I turn to face him.

Seth is leaning against the counter with a beer in his hand. I see anger flare across his face and realize stopping was a bad idea. Before I can turn back to the hallway, he throws the beer can at me. I dodge the can as it splashes over the wall and floor. Then Seth dives at me.

As his right fist connects with my face, I hear him talking. He's saying that it's my fault his world is falling apart.

Chapter 11

Life Lessons

It's been four days since Kenzie went to see Bree. I have texted, phoned and rung her doorbell probably one hundred times since then. Kenzie doesn't answer. I assume Bree told Kenzie the truth about posting the photo and Kenzie has retreated again. Things are back to just like they were before.

My right eye is swollen black and blue. For the three days since the weekend, I've had nothing but people staring at me. My teachers either ignored my face and talked to my shoes, or asked what happened. Being hit with a baseball seemed like the only plausible answer, even though it has been raining too hard for baseball most days. But folks accepted that answer and have left me alone. My dad is MIA. He has no clue what happened. And ever since Seth made me a convenient outlet for his anger, he's actually stayed out of my way.

I don't have any regular classes today. It is the first day of our peer mediator training. I feel an empty pang in my gut. I really wish Kenzie was here with me. I wish I had convinced her to come. I pick an empty seat in the circle and wait for the rest of the students to arrive.

Jessie enters the room and comes to sit beside me. "How's it going?" she asks.

"Could be better. But I am glad to be here."

"Me too."

"Welcome, everyone," says Ms. Golan, the teacher who was with us at the first session.

"We are so glad you're here." By we, I guess Ms. Golan means the older students who helped us before. "Together we will embark on a four-day journey into conflict mediation and how it works. We will share skills you can use to resolve conflicts, and we hope to help you see your strengths. Your teachers picked you because they already know you have the right stuff for helping others. Our hope is that over the next four sessions, you will discover this about yourself, too."

All I can think about is how I failed Kenzie. Will I really learn things to make me a better mediator? Will it help me support my friends? Will it teach me how to help Kenzie? As I'm caught up in my thoughts, Jessie leans in to me. It is the first time I've seen her since the session last week.

"Are you okay?" she whispers, pointing to my eye.

"Ah . . . yeah. Just a baseball. Nothing serious."

"Oh. Sorry that happened."

She turns back to listen to Hudson speaking to all of us. I have a feeling she doesn't believe my lie. Why did everyone else just accept what I told them? What's different about here and now?

Hudson begins to tell us about the importance of understanding the word *harm*, and how conflict causes people to feel hurt. He says our role as mediators is to help people talk about the harm that happened to them when they were in conflict with another. Then our job is to help them figure out how to begin healing that harm.

I turn my thoughts to Kenzie. Cam and Bree caused her harm. My hand rubs the swollen area around my eye. Seth certainly harms me. There is no way my brother's going to change. Especially since losing Bree will hurt his status in the contest. Not to mention how he's also lost Cam.

I didn't expect Cam to fess up. I haven't

talked to Kenzie, so I haven't told her what I overheard yet. But, it does seem as though Cam feels remorse for what he did the night of the party. I don't know if it changes anything for Kenzie. But it's good to know Cam isn't as big a prick as my brother.

Jessie elbows me, signaling it's my turn with the talking piece. We share our message around the circle and then we play a game.

After we've had our movement break, Ms. Golan asks us to move our chairs in front of the screen so we can watch a video. Before Ms. Golan puts the movie on, she lets us know that the show we are about to view has difficult content and can act as a trigger for people's emotions. She tells us we can talk with her, or the older students, if we feel uncomfortable. She also says we can leave if it gets too intense.

I feel uncomfortable as soon as she gives us that message. And the show hasn't even begun yet.

The video is about a teen whose life was taken by another teen. After several years, the parents who lost their son, with help from Fraser Region Community Justice Initiatives in Langley, decide to meet with the young man who took their boy's life. The room is silent as we watch the story unfold on the screen. I hold back tears as they well up inside me.

Parts of this story connect with Kenzie's story — how quickly things can go terribly wrong. How just about anyone can become a victim, or go off the rails and do something horrible. The boy who committed the crime had just aged out of the foster care system. Kenzie doesn't know her dad, and lost her mom because she went to live with some guy she barely knew. And the young man, just like Kenzie, was bullied in school. We learn that alcohol played a part in what happened. There were others present who didn't do anything to stop it. There were bystanders, just like the night of my brother's party.

In the video, we watch as the parents who lost their son meet with the offending teen in prison. They visit and talk with him. They tell him they don't want to hang on to anger. They can see how troubled this youth is. They somehow find a way to forgive him. I don't know if I could do that. Forgiveness takes a ton of courage. I don't know if Kenzie could do that, either. But for the parents and this young man, it made all the difference.

I sit dazed when the show ends. The group leaders suggest a movement break before we discuss what we saw. The idea is to grab some snacks and then come back to talk. I think about the video. I think about how much easier it was when we were younger. I wish we could go back, before things like parties with contests and photos posted on the Internet messed things up. These past two years have been hell.

It's not easy being sixteen.

Chapter 12

Hard Talk

On my way to the snack table, I scan the
room to see how others are reacting to the
video we just saw. People are talking quietly.
Many are making eye contact with each
other. I notice that Huda has left with Ms.
Golan. I remember that she is a refugee.
I imagine she has seen horrors too awful to
speak about. But I guess maybe we have
acts of violence just as horrifying right here
at home.

Most of us are quiet as we bite into our snacks. I drink my apple juice in one long slurp. Then Sean suggests we play a game called Feelings Charades. We have to act out a feeling from a card we draw. The other trainees have to guess what the feeling is. We discover we don't have to act much for the heavy emotions. They are already on the surface. Shame and guilt are tricky to act out. But it makes me think about how these feelings get us stuck in bad places. When my group gets "silly" and "lovestruck," we laugh and it feels good.

When we come back to the circle, Sean begins the discussion with a couple of questions. "Does anyone want to start the conversation? What are your thoughts and feelings about the video we just watched?"

Huda is still not in the room. I remind myself to check in with her later.

Jessie puts her hand out to receive the talking piece. "It reminds me of Amanda Todd," she says.

I hadn't heard of the story in the video, but Amanda Todd's story is still fresh in most of our minds. I remember hearing that Amanda's story was about social media and photos. But I never made the connection to Kenzie. When I first heard about Amanda's story, it was like a blip in a video game. There and gone again.

Thinking about it now, I feel a rumble in my stomach. I figure it's because I wolfed down my snack too fast. But maybe, since we're focused on feelings in our training today, it's also because I feel bad for Amanda. Her story *should* affect all of us. Anyone who uses social media is part of her story.

Jessie continues, "My older cousin went to the same school as Amanda, in Port Coquitlam."

"And how did you feel about Amanda Todd's story when you first heard it?" asks Hudson.

"Well," continues Jessie, "this might sound stupid. But I felt thankful."

No one says anything. But the room gets a weird vibe. Everyone feels disturbed by Jessie's answer. She clarifies, "I mean . . . I was grateful for what her story taught me about the world. My family makes a big deal about being informed. At supper we talk over the day's events. Most of the time, it drives me crazy, especially since we aren't allowed to bring our phones to the table."

The group chuckles. I think of my phone. I realize that in the last few weeks it has been more hassle than staying plugged in is worth.

"Go on," says Ms. Golan. I see she is back in the circle. So is Huda. I smile at Huda and she smiles back.

"Well," says Jessie. "It means we get a chance to sort things out. I had a lot of questions about Amanda's story. Like, how come girls send pictures of themselves to others?"

Suddenly, I feel like I'm going to spill my insides. Jessie's question has hit too close to home.

"Whoa," says a Grade Eleven girl. "I thought you were going to talk about the guys posting pictures. You know, the ones who put pictures up after their girlfriends dump them. How they think they're being cool, sharing them with their buddies."

Then one of the guys pipes up. "I like that we're going to talk about the girls who post pictures. Most of the time we talk about why guys are trading photos. We should look at it from both sides. I'm game to talk about it, as long as we look at all sides of the issue."

Before anyone has a chance to look my way or point fingers at me, I jump out of my seat. I need to get to the washroom.

All the way down the hall, I burp. An awful taste fills my mouth. Once I get to the washroom, I lean over the toilet. But I don't get sick. I just feel like crap. I think of the video, Bree's photo-posting and the stupid contest at my brother's party. All these thoughts churn my insides into an unsettled mush.

I splash my face with cold water. I look in the mirror and try to see the Jared that Mr. Asuni sees, the Jared that Mooney sees, the Jared who can help Kenzie. I need to continue with the mediation training if I'm going to be of any help to Kenzie. Even if it means I get "called out" by my peers. It would still be easier to face than what Kenzie has suffered through. So I head back down the hall toward the library. I fidget in the hall outside for a few moments, getting my courage up.

As I stand there outside the library door, I see Mooney striding down the hall.

"How's it going, bro?" he asks.

My shoulders relax. "Tough. It's good. But it's tough work. We were just talking about Amanda Todd. You remember, the girl who took her own life after some guy posted photos of her online. Sound familiar?"

"Yeah. But in Kenzie's case, it's a girl who did the posting."

"Right — and a former best friend. Maybe that's even worse. Shit. I left Kenzie alone with Bree the other day."

"Bad plan, dude," says Mooney.

"I've tried to reach Kenzie. But she's shut down again. How do I connect with her?"

"Keep trying. I'm sure she knows you're her friend."

"If I hadn't screwed up two years ago, it might be easier to convince her of that."

I sigh as Mooney continues down the hall.

As I enter the library, I hear one of the Grade Ten students speaking. "Okay, now we've talked about Rehtaeh Parsons, too. Two girls who took their own lives after being bullied online over compromising photos. How many people have to die before we figure it out?"

I take a deep breath and grab my seat. I quickly scan the room. No one is looking at me. No one is laying blame in my corner. But I keep a low profile, anyway.

"That's a good question," says Huda. "I hope we don't lose any more lives. But I also know that real change is hard."

"Yeah," adds Jessie. "But I think this is a great start. All of us talking together. I even forgot that we are in different grades. We need to communicate, keep lines open."

I agree with Jessie. But for the rest of the afternoon, I don't add much to the conversation. I just listen and think about how everything relates to Kenzie.

Chapter 13

Delete

As soon as the day is over, I head to Kenzie's house. It seems more important than ever that I should be there to support her.

When I arrive at Kenzie's, I don't bother knocking. She hasn't answered my calls since Saturday. I figure she is shutting the world out and won't let me in anyway. I climb the porch stairs to her front door and pull her key from my pocket. I had meant to put it back after I left Saturday. But in all the confusion,

I completely forgot about it. I turn the handle and quietly enter the house.

The curtains are closed. It's pitch dark. I call out for Kenzie before moving down the hall. I don't want to scare her again. There is no answer. I check the living room. She's not there. I check the kitchen. Same thing. I call her name over and over again as I climb the stairs to the second floor. I move towards Kenzie's room. The door is open a crack.

I push the door wide so I can enter her room. When I see what's there, I feel my mouth fall open.

I crash to the floor beside where Kenzie is lying. She's not moving. My chest heaves like I just fell a thousand feet. Like all the air left my body. I can't catch my breath.

With shaky hands I check Kenzie's wrist for a pulse. Yes! Her heart is beating. She is breathing. But something is not right. Why isn't she awake?

I shake her gently, calling her name. But she

doesn't respond. Now I am freaking out. I open my cellphone. It shakes in my hand as I dial 911.

"Do you require fire, police, or ambulance?" asks the voice on the other end of the phone.

"Ambulance," I whisper. That's as loud as I can make my voice.

"What is the nature of the emergency?"

"My friend . . . she's . . . passed out. I think something happened."

"Does she have a pulse?"

"Yes. But she's not awake or answering me. I just found her. Please, what do I do?"

"I'll dispatch an ambulance. They will be there shortly. Were you with your friend when she became unconscious?"

"No. I just arrived and found her this way."

"Does she appear to have ingested anything?"

"What do you mean?"

"She may have taken a poisonous substance. Or alcohol. Or drugs."

It never dawned on me until now. Maybe Kenzie took something on purpose. Maybe she wanted this to happen. I look around the room. But I don't see anything out of the ordinary. I cover her with the blanket from her bed then go to the bathroom. There is an open pill bottle on the sink ledge.

"I think I found something," I say into the phone.

"Good. What is it?"

"Some pills, in the bathroom. Maybe she took them."

"Can you read the label to me? Is she the one named on the prescription?"

"No," I say, as I read the bottle. "The pills are for her sister Callie." I read the name of the drug to the person on the emergency line. "Are the pills going to kill Kenzie?"

My system floods with panic. I rush back to the bedroom and take Kenzie's hand. It's clammy. With my other hand still holding the cellphone, I listen to the dispatcher.

"What is your friend's full name and how old is she?"

"Kenzie Brown. She's sixteen. When will they get here? Why is it taking so long?"

"Kenzie needs you to be calm, sir. Can you contact her parents to let them know what has happened? They will need to meet her at the hospital."

I can't reach her mom. She never left a forwarding address. We don't know where her dad is. Even if he is living on the reserve in Kamloops, I don't have his number. Kenzie needs her family. I tell the dispatcher I don't know how to get a hold of her parents, but that I will call her sister.

The dispatcher hangs up after she lets me know the ambulance is close by. Right away I punch out the cell number I have for Callie. I hope she hasn't changed the number. I haven't used it since I got it when Kenzie and I were in Grade Nine.

To my relief, Callie picks up. I explain

what has happened, and she says she'll
rush to the Peace Arch Hospital and meet
the ambulance there. I ask her about the
prescription. She says it is a muscle relaxant
prescribed by her doctor to help her sleep after
a car accident. She begins to cry and hangs up.

It's only then that I realize this was on
purpose. Kenzie tried to delete herself.

✳ ✳ ✳

I sit in the hospital waiting room. Callie
doesn't even look my way. She wrings her
hands and stares at the painting on the wall.
It's a picture of a cabin in the woods. It looks
empty and lonely.

I wish Callie would look at me. I am
scared. I'm sure she's scared, too. My knee
bounces and I wish I could focus enough to
read a magazine. I texted Mooney on my way
to the hospital. He was busy, but said he would
try to join me.

After waiting for more than an hour, a hand on my shoulder makes me jump. I look up. It's Mooney. I stand and we hug.

"How are you holding up?" he asks.

"Terrible. I don't know if Kenzie will be okay. I don't know what they're doing to help her." As I crash back into the seat, I notice Callie looking our way.

"I'm glad you went to see her. You probably saved her life," says Mooney. He sits beside me.

"Probably. What if I was too late? How did things get so messed up?" I choke on the last words.

Mooney shakes his head. "I don't know, bro. But I agree. Life is rough."

I put my head between my knees to steady my nerves. I hear a shuffle of feet. I look up to see Callie standing in front of me. She bends down to hug me. Her arms squeeze me tightly. I squeeze back and feel a wave of relief.

"We need to work together to help Kenzie," says Callie.

It's as though she read my mind.

Just then, the Doctor comes out and asks to speak with Callie. They lean against a counter and talk. Mooney and I move closer so we can hear, too.

"She's going to be okay," begins the Doctor.

I feel tears well up in my eyes. I begin to shake. Mooney puts his arm around me until I regain control.

The Doctor continues. "We pumped her stomach. She's alert now, but resting. We'll need to keep her here for a few days for observation."

". . . And so you can help her to get better, right?" I step toward the Doctor so our shoes are almost touching. "So this won't happen again, right?"

He steps back and answers, "Getting better will mostly be up to Kenzie."

I put my hands up in the air. I am about to challenge him, when he continues. "Friends like you will be a big part of her recovery. Be there for her. Show her your support by listening to her. Remind her she isn't alone."

I glance at the picture of the cabin. I don't want Kenzie to think she's alone with all of this. But she may not want my support. Maybe Bree told her I knew that she posted the photo. Maybe Kenzie doesn't feel she can trust anyone.

"You can go in to see her now," the Doctor says to Callie. "But keep it short." The Doctor and Callie shake hands and exchange a few more words.

Then Callie turns to me. "You saved her life, Jared. I can't thank you enough for being there." She places her hand on my shoulder. "I need a few moments on my own first. Then you guys go in."

Mooney nods for the two of us. I don't

know what to say to Kenzie yet, anyway. We sit down to wait for our turn.

"Hey, bro," I say to Mooney. "Will you go in to see her first? Check if she actually wants me there. I caused enough trouble already. I don't want to hurt her again."

"You didn't leave Kenzie, even when she wouldn't answer her phone. You got there in time to make a difference. That says a lot."

"But what if it isn't enough?"

Chapter 14

Un-delete

After what seems like forever, Callie comes out. She says Kenzie will see us. Mooney has to push me to get my legs moving in the direction of Kenzie's hospital room.

Before I focus on Kenzie, I look around the room, which has two beds. In the second bed is a girl about seventeen, reading a magazine. Kenzie's bed is beside the window. It's cloudy outside, so it's dim in the room.

I lean in to Mooney as we approach

Kenzie's bed. I say to him, "Balloons! Remind me to bring bright, colourful balloons next visit. This room is too grey."

"Done," says Mooney. He gets to Kenzie first. He leans in and whispers something to her, then moves aside.

I take three shaky steps. I place my hand on the edge of the bed to steady myself. Kenzie lowers her gaze. Then she begins to shake — just like I was shaking when I heard she was okay.

I break the silence first. "I'm glad I found you."

"Maybe I didn't want to be found," she snaps.

I'm not expecting that. I don't know how to respond. I want to say "that's crazy." But then I think about our training at school. I remember how we talked about shame and embarrassment, guilt and anger.

So instead I say, "Maybe you thought this was the only thing that would make the feelings go away?"

She looks out the window. Then she looks at me. She had the same look on her face when she got caught stealing when we were in Grade Five.

"What is it?" I ask.

"Jared, I screwed up. I didn't mean to . . . I only wanted to sleep. I was alone. There were words flooding my social media pages. I couldn't get them out of my head. I just wanted the noise to stop long enough so I could sleep."

She looks past me. I turn to see that Mooney is heading out the door to give us privacy.

"Jared," she says, "I took my sister's pills. Just a few. I thought they would help me relax. But then I got more anxious. I thought about Bree. I couldn't get that smirk on her face out of my mind. Her words haunted me. Knowing she posted the picture was too much for me to deal with. She even blamed me. And there was the endless stream of posts on the Internet. It was all just too loud in my head. So I took a few more pills. And then, maybe . . ." She rolls her head to the side so I can't see her eyes.

Several minutes pass. It gives me time to think about what Kenzie has said. I take the time to really absorb her words and understand where she's at right now. Finally, I know what to say. I make a connection to the whitewater rafting. "Listen, you survived. Just like you lived through the crazy ride down the rapids."

She sits up and turns her body toward me. "But I'm still in the water, Jared. That's how it feels. Like I can't get my feet on dry land. Like everything is shaky — maybe more shaky than before. A few weeks ago, I thought Bree might be on my side. I was a fool." Kenzie grabs the blanket in her fists and rolls it up toward her. She shakes her head. "That nasty . . . Jesus, she really is a piece of work! I discovered that Seth is sleeping around on her and have proof. So I decided to tell her to drop that bastard brother of yours. When I saw Bree, I felt the old connection to her. I told her I could finally talk to a counselor. I really figured Bree would be on my side."

I put my hand over Kenzie's. Tears make a stream from her eyes to her chin, splashing onto my resting hand.

Kenzie goes on. "I gave Bree way too much credit. She knew about the party and let me go with her. Then, when I told her I was ready to finally tell my story, she posted the photo of me from the party. Where did she even get that picture?"

"From my dumb-ass brother." I can hear the mix of shame and anger in my voice.

"Bree posted it to push me back to a place where I wouldn't be able to act. And it worked."

Kenzie falls silent. I know if I keep her talking, it will make her feel better. "How did you find out about Seth?" I ask.

"Oh, my sister saw your brother at the mall with some other chick. She said his hands were all over her. I told Bree what I knew. Then I bumped into you at Bree's house. That's when Bree told me she posted the photo of me. How could someone be such a good friend and change so much? She even admitted to slut shaming me on social media."

"I think she was angry and jealous. That's why she did those things."

"I guess. You know, back when you asked me out before we started Grade Nine, Bree was upset. I remember her thinking that she'd be the one you'd ask out. She ends up dating Seth. And then I tell her he is cheating on her. I'd be embarrassed, too. Maybe it was partly revenge? Whatever the reason, it's started all over again. This time on social media."

"Maybe Bree started to regret posting all those pictures of herself," I add. "I always thought she did it to keep Seth. But Bree told me she does it for herself."

"Well, Bree put both of us in danger two years ago. And in the end, both of us got hurt.

That's the part I don't get." Kenzie wipes the tears from her eyes.

I take her hand. "I don't get it either. The three of us had such an amazing friendship when we were young — before high school. And now . . . yeah it's different. But maybe it's not a bad thing we know how much Bree has changed. Maybe she isn't someone we need anymore. Maybe we can move forward and rely on each other."

Kenzie squeezes my hand and nods. It wasn't how I planned for her to find out about Bree. But, at least now everything is out in the open.

✹ ✹ ✹

Friday was a professional development day for the province, so there was no school. I spent the day with Kenzie at the hospital. We laughed a lot. I snuck in McDonald's for lunch. Kenzie wanted a toy, so I got her the kid pack. Saturday and Sunday I spent every free minute at the hospital.

Now that I am back at school, I have to wait until the end of the day to visit Kenzie. I haven't seen Mooney, but I know that today he's going to his first GSA meeting. I would join him, except Mr. Asuni grabbed me to help him with the PA system in the gym again.

"Hey, dude," I say as I approach Mooney's locker. "Thanks for everything with Kenzie at the hospital last week. I really needed you there."

"No problem. I was happy to help. How is Kenzie doing?"

"Better, mostly. Bree really did a number on her. Broken trust and all that . . ."

"I get it. But I am glad to hear she isn't shutting you out anymore."

"Me, too!"

Mooney smiles. He lowers his eyes as Colin passes by. Colin stops and turns to us. "Are you planning on attending the meeting today?"

Mooney's cheeks turn red and he stutters, "Yeah . . . I guess."

"Great, come on then." Colin pushes through the throngs of students in the hall to make a path to the resource room.

I turn to Mooney and say, "Later." He nods and heads into the room. There's a goofy grin plastered on his face.

On my way to the gym, I look at the colourful posters lining the walls in the hallway. I think of Kenzie. How she's alone in a grey hospital, with grey gowns and grey food.

Chapter 15

Social Ladder

I arrive at the hospital after school with ten balloons. Each balloon is a different colour so that Kenzie's room will be brighter. My hands shake as I climb the stairs to the second floor. I decided not to take the elevator. The stairs help me use up some of my nervous energy. Each time I go to visit, I don't know what to expect. Will Kenzie be happy, sad, or depressed? Will she still want me to hang out?

When I get to Kenzie's room, the bed is

empty. The sheets are pulled back. A big stuffed polar bear leans against her pillow.

"She'll be back soon," says the girl in the other bed. "We just finished our art therapy session. Kenzie stayed in the room to work on something."

"Oh, thanks," I reply. I wander to the window and look out. Not a great view — mostly the parking lot and houses. I anchor the balloons on the tray beside her bed. Some leftover mystery meat is in one segment of the tray. But the other two slots are empty. One looks like it might have held mashed potatoes.

"Hey, Jared." Kenzie's voice sends a warm wave through me. She sounds upbeat. I turn and hug her as she reaches the bed. She lets me keep my arms around her for a few moments. Then she notices the balloons.

"Awesome! Thanks." She picks up a fluorescent green one. She ties the string around her wrist to cover her hospital name band. She pulls her robe tighter and fiddles with her hair.

"I just came by to bring the balloons. And to see how you are doing," I say.

"I'm pretty good," she says. "I met with my counselor again this morning. We've been meeting every day since I've been here. When I go home, we'll meet once a week. This afternoon, we had art therapy. Instead of painting or drawing, I wrote a poem. The facilitator said whatever helps us tap into our emotions is good. So that's what I did."

"Can I read it?" I ask. Poetry isn't my thing. But it seems important to Kenzie and I want to be there for her.

"I don't think I'm ready to share it, yet."

"I get it."

"But I will tell you what I was thinking about when I wrote it," says Kenzie. "I was thinking about high school and the social ladder you have to climb to fit in. You know, the one where Bree figures she's already at the top?"

"Yeah," I say. "But, I don't get why she thinks that. Looks aren't everything."

"They are to Bree. And to guys like your brother."

"Then let them have each other," I reply. My blood heats up thinking about Seth.

"But that's where I screwed up," says Kenzie. "I tried climbing the social ladder behind Bree. I gave in to the pressure from her and from everyone else, the pressure to be someone I'm not. Anyone who thinks I should look a certain way and act a certain way, just to fit in."

"Like me? I was a jerk."

"Actually, Jared, not you. Not in this case. I've had time this past week to do a lot of thinking. You were one of the few people who liked me for who I was. You liked me even though I was afraid of whitewater rafting. You liked me even though I liked roasting marshmallows over the campfire better than setting up the tent. And you even liked me in jeans and a tee."

"You always looked great. You still look

great." I feel a flush run up to my neck and cheeks. Maybe I'm the same shade of red Mooney was when Colin took him to the GSA meeting. Kenzie doesn't notice as she has her head down.

"But I got caught up in thinking I needed to be popular. I wanted the attention Bree was getting. My counselor said a lot of how I acted has to do with my mom taking off. It was only a year after she bailed on us that I went to the party. Maybe things would be different if . . ."

She doesn't finish the sentence. Instead, she climbs back in bed. She pulls the covers over her housecoat. She tucks the polar bear stuffy between her arms so she's hugging it close to her chest. A giant yawn escapes her mouth. I copy her, but my jaw cracks as I take in a long, deep breath.

"Do you mind if I rest for now, Jared?" she asks. "Today's activities have wiped me out. My sister will come after she gets off work, so I'll have company tonight. Will you come visit me tomorrow?"

"Of course." I lean in. Without thinking, I kiss her cheek.

* * *

At home I open a can of chili and warm it up on the stove. I spread two pieces of bread with garlic butter and throw them into the toaster oven. While I wait for my dinner to heat up, I get a text from Mooney.

Mooney: OMG. Colin is amazing!

Me: Still at school?

Mooney: No, just had coffee with Colin.

Me: R u going out again?

Mooney: You bet!

Me: Happy 4 u.

Mooney: Thumbs up!

As the chili begins to bubble, I turn it down. I reach into the cupboard for a bowl. As I turn off the toaster oven, my phone beeps with another text.

Mooney: Talking to Mom tonight. Colin gave
    me ideas. Wish me luck.

Me: Want me there?

Mooney: Gotta do this on my own. But thnx!

Me: U got this!

Mooney: Keep u posted.

It will be tough for Mooney to talk to his family. I feel a wave of pride for my friend.

I grab a chair and sit at the table with my food. I think about how Kenzie was brave and talked to Bree. Before the photo surfaced, she was ready to talk about that painful night. Now Mooney is going to come out to his parents. I wish I had their courage.

I have had a few bites of food when my dad arrives with Laurel. They say "Hi" and head into the living room. I hear the news come on the TV. I hear Dad and Laurel talking with each other.

I don't know what makes me do it. But I get out of my chair and join them in the living room.

"Jared, what's going on?" Dad asks.

"Jeez! Wouldn't it have been nice if you asked that when you came through the kitchen? Anything . . . like, how's your day going? How's your life going?"

"Do we have to get into this right now?" He nods toward Laurel like I should be quiet and leave the adults alone.

It only fuels my anger. "Do you have any idea what the last two years have been like for me? What the last few weeks have been like? I've been going through hell. And you are out playing with your girlfriend, acting like a teenager!"

Dad says to Laurel, "I'm sorry for my son's behaviour."

"*My* behaviour! Try taking a look at your own behaviour. Some role model you are!"

I march back to the kitchen. I've lost my appetite. I scrape the chili into the garbage. Some splashes onto the white cupboard.

It looks like blood as it drips.

Chapter 16

Halloween

It's been a week since I yelled at my dad. It's Halloween. I'm on my way to the hospital to see Kenzie after school again. I missed connecting with Mooney today, so I text him as I walk.

Me: What's up?

Mooney: Talking to Dad today.

Mooney told me that his mom had been totally cool when he shared his news with her. He was relieved. But he wanted to wait before telling his dad.

Me: How do u do it? How do u find the
courage?

Mooney: Same way I did with Mom. Just jump
in and say the 1st words. Then there is no
turning back. No matter what happens. U
helped 2. By supporting me.

Me: Your mom supports u — your dad will 2.

Mooney: Thanks. Still nervous . . .

Me: On my way to see Kenzie. Do u think
she'll ever find the courage again? To talk
about what happened 2 yrs ago?

Mooney: Fear stopped me from talking to my
folks. Fear has kept Kenzie quiet 2.

Me: I wish courage came in a pill.

I'm walking the last block to the hospital.
I think about telling Kenzie what I learned in
training today. I wonder if I might use some of
the skills we practiced. We talked about "heart
listening" and empathy.

I think my dad must be low on the
empathy scale, or he wouldn't treat me like I'm
not there. I know Seth is devoid of empathy. If

he had any, he wouldn't have held a party with a contest to see how many Grade Nine girls the Grade Twelve jerks could sleep with. And he wouldn't be doing it still — challenging guys to host parties, getting girls to share pictures of themselves. And Bree? Well, Bree's too involved with herself to care about her friendships.

I know one thing for sure. I don't want to be like any of them.

When I arrive at Kenzie's hospital room, she is coming back from art therapy again.

"Hey, Jared. Good to see you."

"You, too." I can see that Kenzie is getting stronger. Her hair is cut and her big brown eyes are visible. They aren't so vacant, and they even seem to sparkle. She has more energy than she had before. She takes my hand and leads us down the hall to a sitting room. We each grab a recliner and push the button so we are leaning back. No one else is in the room. It's rare to get privacy in the hospital.

"Where's your roommate?" I ask.

"Oh, she went home. Someone new arrived yesterday. She's a twelve-year-old girl. I think she has an eating disorder or something. She's a toothpick. I feel bad for her. She's so young."

Kenzie has empathy. Especially for another person who is in a tough spot. Kenzie knows about being in tough spots.

"I bet you'll be a good influence for her."

She reaches for my hand. "Thanks for being here, Jared."

I nod. "I just wish I had been there when you needed me the most."

"You are here now. And about the past, I get it," she says. "Seth is a big jerk. Emphasis on BIG. I saw your bruises. Even though I didn't say anything, I knew they had to be from your brother."

"I still should have warned you before that night. I shouldn't have worried about what would happen to me."

"Truth be told," Kenzie bows her head, "I probably wouldn't have listened to you. I had my mind set. I'd done my hair that morning. I had an outfit I just purchased from the used clothing store by my house. I was ready to take off down the popular path. Even though you were waiting for me."

"I was."

"I know. I wish I had focused on all our good times together. You and I had fun when we started dating. We were close. We were friends first. That made it that much better. And I had to go and ruin it, by taking . . ."

"The 'popular path,'" I finish.

"I wish I hadn't given a damn about being popular."

"I get it though," I say. "You were friends with Bree first, before you and I knew each other. Wasn't it like Grade Two when you guys met?"

Kenzie nods.

I continue, "So, you wanted her to see you

as someone who could keep up — someone who fit in with her."

"Except," laughs Kenzie, "I thought she was connected to loads of people. I see now that most people don't like her. They aren't near her for friendship. They just want status, too. So, they all say and do the things Bree says and does. I'm sad that it took me so long to figure it out."

"I'm just glad you did. Now you can be you again!"

Kenzie holds my hand. We sit that way in the silent room, watching the sky darken through the window.

"How long will you be staying here?" I ask as we return to Kenzie's room. The food trays are going around. Kenzie climbs in bed as a nurse sets a tray on the bedside table. It looks like roast beef and baked potato. The green Jell-O wiggles.

"Just until Friday. Then I go home."

I feel a wave of panic. Sure, Kenzie is

stronger now. But what about when she gets home?

Kenzie hasn't had access to her phone since she's been in the hospital. It wasn't on her when the ambulance came. And even though Kenzie has asked Callie non-stop to bring it to her, Callie has refused. Callie figures that Kenzie will heal more quickly without the steady stream of negative messages from the Internet. I agree. But now Kenzie will be home and have access to her phone. Have the messages stopped? Will there be new ones? What about school?

All these thoughts are zipping around in my head. Kenzie takes my hand. "Did you hear me, Jared?"

"No, sorry, what did you say?"

"That I want you to know I am going to be okay. But I'm worried about catching up on my core subjects. We have provincial exams coming up soon."

"I can help you study. Except for Social

Studies. I am getting good grades in all my other classes."

"Right on," she says. She finishes off the Jell-O. But she hasn't touched the other food.

My stomach growls.

"Want some of my meat?" She offers me a bite of her roast beef. Funny how it looks good, but it tastes like cardboard.

"I guess I should get going," I say. "I have a ton of homework. But here, I got you something — for Halloween."

"Oh my gosh. I totally forgot it's Halloween."

I open my knapsack and pass Kenzie something that looks like a skeleton hand. It's actually popcorn stuffed into one of those clear disposable gloves people wear when they prepare food. She laughs and unties the top to get at the popcorn. Then she giggles as she notices the green plastic ring I put inside one of the fingers. She slides it onto her finger.

I smile. "I wish we could have had a party

tonight like we used to. Halloween was always our favourite holiday."

"I couldn't have handled a party, Jared."

"I meant just a party of two. We could have watched videos and eaten popcorn. So what costume would you have picked to wear, if we did?"

"I have to think . . ." She looks out the window.

Why can't I plan a party for two? She'll be going home soon. I figure it might be tough being back in her house, back where she almost killed herself.

"What if we have our own belated Halloween?" I say. "We can dress up this weekend. Watch movies and eat tons of chocolate!"

She laughs. "Only I want the boxes of Smarties — all of them!" Then she tilts her head like she is thinking of something. "I have an idea for my costume," she says. "Maybe I'll wear a square frame around my face."

"*What?*" I ask.

"You know — a frame. Like one that goes around a picture. That way I can make a picture of me. The real me."

I smile. Kenzie pushes the food out of her way and grabs a pen and paper.

"Sorry, Jared. But I just got an idea for another poem. Maybe I'll send it to you when it's ready."

I leave the hospital thinking about Kenzie's real face in a picture frame.

That's a lot better than the last picture everyone saw of her.

Chapter 17

Force-fields

It is the first weekend in November. Kenzie is home. We have decided to spend Saturday afternoon together watching movies. My stomach is growling for food. I open my phone to nothing from Kenzie or Mooney. But on my social media page is a new batch of slanders against Kenzie. What the hell? Can't those losers let it go? I bet Bree is behind it. She probably knows Kenzie is home from the hospital. What is her problem?

I'm about to step into the shower when a wave of panic hits me. What if Kenzie sees the nasty messages? What if she isn't strong enough yet? What if this pushes her over the edge again?

I skip the shower and run back to my room. I jump into fresh clothes. I don't check my hair. I just grab my coat and fly out the door. My feet carry me to Kenzie's house. I bang on the door. I can feel my heart beating in my fingers. I'm scared of what I'll find. I can't catch my breath.

Kenzie opens the door. She's still in her pajamas. She has bedhead, like me. I let out my breath, happy that she opened the door. Happy that she is still alive.

"Jared, what's wrong?" she asks, looking alarmed. "You look like you saw a ghost. Halloween was last week. What's up?"

I grab Kenzie and pull her into my arms. I must be squeezing too tightly because she says, "Jared, let go. It hurts."

"Sorry." I drop my arms and step back.
I look her up and down. "I'm just glad you're
okay. I'm so glad you're here."

Kenzie invites me into the front hall where
I take off my shoes. Then I follow her into the
living room. The fish tank bubbles with clear
water. The fish seem to swim happily. I flop
down onto the couch saying, "I was worried . . .
I thought maybe you had hurt yourself again."

Her eyes widen. She sees why I am at her
house early, and in a panicked state.

"Jared," she says, "I'm fine. What made
you think I'd hurt myself again?"

"I saw some stuff on social media. I thought
you might have seen it, too."

"Hey, you don't need to worry. With
catching up on school work, writing poetry,
your friendship and my sister's support,
I don't need that other crap. I haven't even
checked my cell or tablet. And I don't plan to.
I'm in a better place, Jared. I'm beginning
to heal."

I take Kenzie's hand as she sits beside me. "Okay," I say. "I feel better now." I grab my phone and punch out a text. "I'm just sending Mooney a message. As I was running down the street, I sent him a note to meet me here. I guess I was acting out of fear of what I thought may have happened." I chuckle with relief.

Mooney texts back with a thumbs-up emoji.

"Crap, Jared," complains Kenzie.

"Hey, at least Mooney cares about you . . . like me."

"True, he's been a good friend."

"So," I say. I tuck my phone back into my pocket. "I keep forgetting to ask. What did Mooney whisper to you that first day in the hospital?"

"Oh, he said that he gets scared too. He thinks that he and I are both lucky. We're lucky to have someone in our life who cares about us. You."

"And here I was thinking it was something deep," I sigh.

"Well, it might not be deep. But it is important," replies Kenzie. "We do have you. Now that you and I are talking again, it really makes a difference. Thanks."

Kenzie leans in to kiss my cheek. She lingers for a moment, like maybe she will kiss my lips. But then she pulls back. I know that she might not ever want us to be more than friends. I'll respect her wishes and follow her lead.

"Jared, since you're here anyway, why don't we start our movie marathon now? I can make us lunch. You can figure out what we should watch."

Kenzie gets up and heads to the kitchen. It's still early for lunch. But I didn't eat breakfast, so I'm famished. I find leftover scary movies from Halloween, but I decide to skip over all of them. Even though watching them would be a blast, I figure life has been scary enough this past while. Instead, I pull up the original *X-Men* movies. Kenzie and I are both still into superheroes. I can see from Kenzie's history that she recently watched *Elektra*. Maybe watching Wolverine and Storm defeat evil and triumph over Magneto will be just what we need.

Kenzie calls me to the kitchen to help carry out the food. She's made our old staple: grilled cheese sandwiches, potato chips and root beer floats. I smile as I see the straw sticking out of the foam at the top of the float. We crash onto the couch. As soon as Kenzie sees what I've picked she says, "Perfect!"

We settle in for hours of movies. Before we begin, I say to Kenzie, "Next year for Halloween, you should dress as the mutant, Polaris." I read all the Marvel comics to Kenzie when we were younger. It's like our own language, our own story.

"Why would I want to be her? She lost her powers on M-Day."

"Right," I say, "but she learned how to create force-fields. Now she can protect herself from evil."

"Force-fields. You are so right! I need to learn how to create force-fields around myself." She dips her sandwich in ketchup. She looks up and smiles, her mouth full of food. We both laugh and it feels good.

"You know, " I add, "You *are* a superhero. Dealing with what happened to you. I know things got freaky for a while. But you've pulled out of that space. You're here and you are working things out."

"It's a long process, Jared. I'll have lots of down days still. And I have so much to work through. With my counselor's help, I can look back and see what happened. I can start to understand some of the things that brought me down."

"Like what?"

"A big stress for me was losing my mom the way I did. She had a choice. But she chose some guy she barely knew over her two daughters. The counselor helped me to see how hurt I was, and I guess how angry I felt over her betrayal."

"So you went to the party because of your mom?"

"Not exactly. Just, it made me make some bad choices. Maybe I didn't care about myself that much. My mom gave up on me and Callie. And I guess I kind of gave up on myself. I took a bad risk. That night ruined me. I never thought I'd get past it. But I am slowly healing."

I take a sip of my float and some of the foam goes up my nose. My choking breaks the tension between us. But only for a moment.

Kenzie changes the focus of the conversation to me. "You were right to be mad at me for putting myself at risk. For dissing you that night. I made that choice, just like my mom made hers. I wrecked what we had by thinking I needed some older guy to feel important."

I take a deep breath. I want to just turn the movie on now. We can't go back and I'm letting the past go. So I say, "Let's forget about it. Let's start fresh. We are rebuilding our friendship. And we've got these awesome floats and sandwiches and leftover Halloween candy. Let's relax and enjoy the show."

Kenzie agrees. We press play.

Chapter 18

Memories

After the third movie, Kenzie falls asleep with her head resting in my lap. I think about everything that's happened over the past month. I think about the picture of Kenzie with her eyes closed.

I shudder as I remember Seth's voice from that night. He tried to justify what he and Cam did by saying, "The girls were hot. And they were up for it." Ha! Maybe Bree was, but not Kenzie.

I am not that kind of guy. These past few weeks, I've been reminded of my friendship with Kenzie and how much I care about her. To me, she's a lot more than just how she looks. Isn't that how it's supposed to be?

I grab the blanket from the back of the couch and pull it up over Kenzie's shoulders. After several minutes, I feel my eyes drooping, heavy with sleep.

I am startled awake by Callie's keys in the door. I sit up abruptly and Kenzie stirs. She is still asleep in my lap. But her eyes begin to open. She yawns and sits up as Callie enters the living room.

We must have slept for a long time. Callie is already finished her shift at work.

"I brought home pizza," Callie says. "What are you watching? Is there room on the couch for me?"

"Absolutely," says Kenzie with a big grin on her face.

When I finally leave around midnight,

Kenzie leans in for a hug as I reach the front door. We linger in the hug. Our cheeks touch as we pull apart. I smile and head out into the crisp night air.

The last few days have been wet and rainy. But as I leave Kenzie's house, the clouds have parted. The moon is bright. A few stars shine.

I hope Kenzie is looking out her window to see the shooting star that just blazed across the sky.

* * *

It's Remembrance Day, and there is no school. That's why I'm already on the ferry heading to see my mom. She is still staying with my aunt, but will be moving into her boyfriend's house soon. It's my mom's birthday today. I look at her unwrapped present. It's a charm for her bracelet. I got it at the mall in the jewelry store. It took a good chunk out of my savings, but I know my mom will love it.

I've decided I'm cool with her moving in with Steve. She's happier and seems to have resolved the past stuff with my dad.

We meet my aunt in downtown Nanaimo, at a service to honour the veterans. My great-grandpa fought in the Korean War. As we observe a moment of silence to remember the fallen soldiers, I think about how lately it has been a war zone in my own life.

My best friend suffered through date rape and two years of silence by herself. I see now that I was a bystander to what happened to Kenzie, like the guys in the video we saw in our training session. I wasn't in the room when it happened, but I could have prevented it. I could have spoken up after it happened. I was afraid, and my fear made it tougher for Kenzie to heal. In that moment of silence, I make a promise to Kenzie — to talk, if she can't.

Mom takes my hand as the bagpipes play. Then we head back to my aunt's house and Mom makes us lunch. She sits down and takes a bite of her corned beef sandwich. She looks at me with sadness in her eyes.

I say, "You're thinking about your grandpa, right?"

She nods. Then her expression changes to one of concern. She places her hand beside my eye. She rubs my cheek.

"Jared, what is that?" Mom brushes my face again and I pull away. With the back of my hand, I rub my eye. I've got so used to it. I forgot that the bruise from Seth left a residue of yellow. I didn't think it was even noticeable anymore.

"Jared, did someone hit you?" Mom presses.

It's funny how a holiday like Remembrance Day can bring up a host of old memories. I think about the day after Bree broke up with Seth and Cam called him out. That day my brother was the most violent he'd ever been with me. I think about how my dad has been too absent to notice the bruise. And in this moment, I realize how much I miss my mom. A stupid tear rolls down my cheek. I lower my head.

"Jared, what's wrong? That is a bruise, isn't it? Who gave it to you? Did someone at school do this?"

I can't put my thoughts into words. So I just shake my head.

"Did someone in the community do this to you?"

Again, I shake my head.

"Then who? Please, Jared. Talk to me."

Then it's like I'm channelling Mooney. I feel Mooney's courage. If he can come out to his folks, I should be able to tell my mom what's been happening. Kenzie's counselor talked about how her mom taking off affected her. In a way, my mom bailed, too. Even though I get why, I missed having her around.

I take a huge breath and jump in. "Mom, the bruise is from Seth. In fact, he's hurt me loads of times since you left — since that stupid party of his. You know how he's always picked on me, but now he's more aggressive. He's more physical. I've actually been scared."

"I'm sorry, Jared." Mom puts her hand over mine. "I should have been there for you. After that night, I was so upset, I ran away from the problem. But you were never the problem. I never meant to run away from you."

"I get why you left, Mom. I guess if I had been brave, I would have asked to come with you. But I was used to my school and my friends. And I hoped Dad would do more. I guess I thought he'd be a parent."

"I assumed your dad was there for you. This is not acceptable. I'm phoning him right now. How could he not tell me about your bruise? What was he thinking?"

"Don't call him, Mom. He isn't home enough to notice anything. It will just piss him off. It will make things worse. I can't deal with that right now. Especially with everything going on with Kenzie."

"What happened with Kenzie?"

I tell my Mom everything, starting with the party. I finish with sharing that Kenzie is seeing a counselor and is home from the hospital. By this time my Mom is crying. I hand her a box of tissues.

"Jared," she says, "I am so sorry. I let my pain get in the way of seeing that you were hurting. I missed the signs that you were upset about more than just losing our family. At the time, I thought you'd be happier with your dad. You know, male bonding and all that."

I chuckle. "I can't bond with my brother, or my dad. We are just too different."

"Jared, I really let you down."

". . . And I let Kenzie down."

We hug. Mom asks if she can help Kenzie. She asks what Kenzie plans to do. I explain that Kenzie is close to fixing things — on her own. Mom also wants to talk to my dad. I can't stop her. But I know I have to face him at some point. *I* have to tell him how I feel. Mom says she'll respect my wishes and wait for that time.

Relief courses through me. I go for a walk around my aunt's house to clear my head. I decide to text Kenzie. I need to tell her that I realize now I was a bystander. I can set things up and be her voice, but only if she needs me to help share her story.

Me: How r u?

Kenzie: Good. How's your Mom?

Me: Ready for her big move.

Kenzie: I'm happy for her. She's getting her life back. U know, I didn't cut u any slack after the party. Your Mom moved away and u were on your own.

Me: I'm dealing with it.

Kenzie: Hey, since it's Remembrance Day, I'm thinking about us before the party. How good we were together. Also how I was ready to face things and move on. I'm not there yet. Maybe with time, I can get back to that place?

Me: I will help u — whatever it takes — whatever u need.

Kenzie: I know. Thanks! ☺

Chapter 19

Gifts

I will be spending Christmas in Nanaimo with Mom and Steve. So I head to Kenzie's place for a celebration of our own. It's the 23rd of December. Even though it has snowed in the past few days, most of the white stuff is melting with the rain. The snowman Kenzie and I made in her front yard is leaning over sideways. I try to prop him up before I knock on her door.

Kenzie has baked chocolate chip cookies. I bring pop and a chicken dinner from the store. It has two salads and French fries along with the whole chicken. Before we eat, I raise my glass of pop to make a toast.

"Kenzie, to your first week back at school. Now you can chill for a while before we start next semester."

"Yeah," Kenzie says, sipping her pop. "I'm glad for the break. My counselor thought it would be a good idea to try a week before Christmas. Just see how it feels being at school full-time again. I have to admit, it was tough. I tried to channel my superpowers. Creating a force-field around myself at school is not easy."

We laugh together. But I can see how being back at school has affected Kenzie. She has circles under her eyes again. She's letting her hair grow to cover her face. Maybe over the break she'll gain enough strength to make the school transition in January easier.

After we have chowed down, we move to the living room. The fish tank bubbles and I can see Kenzie has cleaned it again. She has draped a shiny green garland around the tank. It looks festive for the fish. The tree I brought her last week twinkles with multi-coloured lights. I place my present for Kenzie under the tree.

I clear my throat and begin. "Kenzie, before we open our presents, I want to tell you I'm sorry. I know now what you meant when you said I wanted to get rid of my guilt. You were right. I didn't see how damaging my actions were. I stood by, knowing why my brother was having the party. But I didn't tell you. That was unfair to you. I put you at risk. And for the longest time, I did blame you for going to the party. I see that wasn't fair either. You hoped for attention from the Grade Twelve guys. But no one wants THAT kind of attention."

Kenzie puts her present to me under the tree. She doesn't look my way. But from where I am standing, I can see a tear rolling down her cheek.

"Thanks, Jared. Now we're good. Now it's easier to see that part of my struggle was because I wasn't talking about the party. I told my sister. And she stayed with me. I told you. And we've had some bumps along the way. But now you are here by my side. My counselor from the hospital knows what happened."

She pauses, then goes on. "I have a long way to go to trust people again. But I do want to tell my story. Sometime. Maybe in the New Year? Maybe I will make it my New Year's resolution. Then I'll have to follow through."

"Like you said before," I remind her, "you don't have to do anything. But I will be at your side, whatever you decide."

Kenzie stands and takes my hand. She leads me to the couch to sit down. I open my phone and turn on some tunes. I've already turned off the living room lights, so we are sitting in the glow of the Christmas tree.

"So, are you going to frame your certificate? The one you received for finishing the mediation training?" Kenzie smiles.

"I don't think so!" I laugh. "I will keep it for my resume. But seriously, it was great timing, having the training now. It helped me think about what happened to you. It made me look at my relationship with Dad and Seth. It's funny, I thought at first the training would help me fix things. You know, make everything better."

"Life's not like that," says Kenzie. She loops her fingers through mine.

"Sure isn't." I shake my head. "For the longest time, I hoped I could find the courage to talk to my dad and Seth. But I am pretty sure they aren't in a place where they can be sorry or change their behaviour. If I try talking to them, I'll probably get pissed off because they won't get it. It's not worth it. The training taught me that mediation isn't supposed to hurt people more."

"So, what are you going to do?"

"Maybe I'll think about what I *would* say to

them, if I felt they would listen. Maybe I don't have to hear them say they're sorry. Maybe I just need to say it to myself — to heal, you know? Like you said, you've heard me. I've told you what my family is like. Mom now knows about Seth. So maybe I am working it out already." Even as I say the words, I feel better. Some of the load has been lifted off my shoulders.

"That makes a lot of sense," replies Kenzie. "It's about finding your voice, even if you don't use it toward the people who hurt you. My counselor says my poetry has become a way of saying what I haven't been able to say out loud. My poetry is my voice."

I nod.

Kenzie goes on. "All I really want is to be heard. I want to say all the words that have been in my head for the past two years. I want to express every thought no one heard, every feeling I pushed down. I want everyone to know the fear I have lived with, I just want it all out in the open."

"Anything you need from me, just say it!" I can make that promise.

"Well, if I decide at some time to confront Cam, would you be there for me?"

"Are you kidding? Of course!"

She nods. "Whatever I decide, it would help a lot to have you there for support. Not to say the words for me. I have to be the one to express what's inside me. Just to hold my hand so I can find my voice."

"Done!"

I want Kenzie to unwrap her gift. But I haven't shared the best part of my news yet. "So, guess what?"

"Hmm?"

"I don't have to worry about being pulverized by Seth anymore. He's moving out! He's going to share an apartment with some dude from work."

Kenzie squeezes my hand. "That's awesome news, Jared. Now you'll be safe. And ever since you told me what you overheard Cam saying to your brother, I've felt a sense of hope. Maybe things are looking up for both of us?"

Kenzie hugs me. Then she slides over to the tree and picks up a small, wrapped package. As she hands it to me, she says, "I got you something small. I went to the mall by myself. Even though I ducked into stores every time I saw someone from school, I didn't bolt. I got presents for you and Callie."

"Thanks for doing this. It means a lot."

I open the package. In it is a pair of black gloves. When we built our snowman, I used the only gloves I could find at home. They were full of holes. My hands were frozen. I try on the new gloves. "These are perfect!" I hug Kenzie, then pass her my gift. I don't say a word. I don't have to.

Her eyes light up when she removes the paper and sees the label on the box. "A camera. Wow!"

"With this, you can control what pictures are taken. Pictures of you or anyone else."

When I decided on the camera, I hoped it might help Kenzie get back to her true self. I add, "And it's better than the camera on your phone. You don't have to have your phone on to take a picture. You won't have that constant pinging from jerks weighing in on your life. What do they know about you — the real you?"

Kenzie hugs me. Once she gets the camera out of the package, she snaps about forty shots. She takes pictures of me and then the two of us together.

Then she smiles. She turns the camera on herself and takes a self-portrait.

A Note from the Author

Fraser Region Community Justice Initiatives in Langley, B.C., runs a four-day training session for students to learn about restorative practices and to become peer mediators. They also facilitate victim/offender mediations. While the story of the two boys is not true, CJI Langley helps with situations just like the one in this novel. For more information on the programs they offer, please check out their website: http://www.cjibc.org.
Additional resources:

kidshelpphone: http://www.kidshelpphone.ca/teens/home.aspx

Kelty Mental Health Resource Centre:
http://keltymentalhealth.ca/

http://www.mcf.gov.bc.ca/mental_health/links.htm

And school personnel, especially counselors, are there to help you and to suggest local and community support systems.

Acknowledgements

Thanks to the great team at Lorimer and especially my amazing editor Kat, who went beyond and above this time around! YOU are a superhero!

A special thanks to Dan Basham, Kaylie Maughan and the fabulous team at the Fraser Region Community Justice Initiatives for all your hard work in inspiring and supporting Peer Mediators in Langley Schools, and for your work in the community. I have learned so much from all of you and you have inspired me!